MARS HILL

DIRK VAN HOUTEN

Copyright © 2020 by Dirk van Houten

All rights reserved. The moral rights of the author have been asserted.

No part of this book may be reproduced in any form or by any electronic or mechanical means, including information storage and retrieval systems, without written permission from the author, except for the use of brief quotations in a book review. All rights reserved.

This is a work of fiction. Names, characters, and incidents either are the product of the author's imagination or are used fictitiously. Any resemblance to actual persons, living or dead, events, or locales is entirely coincidental.

Proudly published by Six Cats Press, Alberta Canada

ISBN: 978-1-7772331-1-2 - Print

ISBN: 978-1-7772331-0-5 Digital

1

I woke up to the thud of the landing gear touching down at the airport in Phoenix.

Despite sleeping for the three and a bit hour flight from Chicago down to Arizona, I was still exhausted. Yet, once we were on the ground, my misgivings melted, and I smiled at the view from the plane's window. The cloudless sky was bluer than I had ever seen it, and the sun was bright. Heat radiated from the pavement as the plane turned from the runway and moved toward the gate. The workers around the terminal wore shorts and T-shirts—this surprised me since it was March, and snow still lay on the ground back home.

I let out a low moan as I stretched. Being six-foot-four, my knees and back were killing me from the cramped seating on the plane. It was an enormous relief when we finally parked at the gate, and I could stand and move around. I grabbed my backpack from under the seat in front of me as I stood, releasing all the strain on my back. Soon, I was in the slow line of people heading toward the plane's door. I stopped to say thank you to the flight attendant and pilot. As

I stepped onto the jetway, a blast of heat hit me like a ton of bricks. It wasn't that hot, really, but after arriving from Chicago in March, it was warmer than I expected. It irked me to feel relieved at the first burst of air conditioning in the airport concourse. After all, coming from winter on the lakes, the warmth should have been a relief, right?

"Jeremy!" my Aunt Gillian shouted when she saw me walking down the stairs into the baggage hall. She carried a coffee in one hand and handed me a large tea from the other. A lock of her long red hair had fallen across her pale face, and she kept trying to blow it away, with little success. I rushed forward and grabbed my cup, freeing up a hand for her to tuck the stray hair behind her ear.

"Thanks, Aunt G. Nice to see you. How is Aunt Sam?" I asked, giving her a one-armed hug before taking a careful but large swallow of hot tea. "I'm surprised you remembered that I prefer tea," I said, as the warm and bitter taste of the liquid warmed my mouth.

"Course I did, Jer. The last time you drank coffee, you threw up all over my cookies, remember? Sam's fine. She's super-excited about our new cat, Luthien. Like I always say—"

"—Cats are better than kids," we said together, laughing at the old family joke. My aunt was also a super Tolkien fan, like me. It didn't surprise me that she named the cat after the famous elf maiden who had given up mortality to live with her human soulmate. Aunt Gillian liked to pretend the story was about her and Aunt Sam.

Almost a decade ago, Aunt G had introduced Samantha to the family. My grandmother had asked how Aunt G would give her more grandkids. Aunt G just smiled and said she could have grand kitties, and that cats were better than kids, anyway. Having an annoying set of twins as younger siblings myself, I could agree with that.

"I can't wait to meet the elf maiden cat. Are you working tonight?" I asked, grabbing my bag from the carousel and heading toward the parking lot.

"Yep. Got up early to make the drive down here to pick you up."

"Hope it wasn't any trouble."

"How could I not come to pick up my favorite college student?"

Aunt Gillian was an astronomer at the Lowell Observatory. She also instructed at Northern Arizona University in Flagstaff, the city where I was to spend the next six months. She had done her doctorate work at Lowell, and once she graduated, they had hired her. Mom told me it was something to do with how she was a hot-shot astrophysicist, and that she had lots of places looking for her. I had paid little attention at the time to what Aunt Gillian researched. Now that I would spend time here, I would have to make sure I found out.

My parents sent me out here after a health crisis during my first year at the University of Chicago. They and my doctors had decided it would be in my best interest to take a break from school. They wanted me to go somewhere with good, warm air, clear skies, and plenty of healthy sunscreen-protected sunshine. So, Aunt G pulled a few favors and got me a job working for the interpretive center that the observatory ran at their Mars Hill site.

Aunt G and I shot the shit on the two-hour drive up to Flagstaff. Any intention of finding out what she researched left my mind as the tea and good company made me chatty. Traffic sucked until we were well clear of Phoenix but then eased up on the highway as we headed north. The closer we got, the more I could see summer turn back to winter, snow starting to fall in shadows cast on the ground.

We spent the time on the road catching up on news and talking about girls—or, more precisely, how I didn't have any in my life. Being sick and missing most of the scholastic experiences that your friends took part in leads to not having many friends in short order, much less a girlfriend, or even a real honest date. The reputation of someone who's sick all the time also hung over my head. When people know you are sick, they either coddle you, or they avoid you as though you're contagious.

After we hit the exit into Flagstaff, traffic was as bad as it ever got in this small town, or so Aunt G told me. But nothing compared to Chicago or even Phoenix. So, when Aunt G complained about waiting for twenty seconds to make a left turn, I just laughed.

We finally turned down a little street at the base of a hill covered in trees. I had never been here before, and I worried about culture shock—I wasn't used to being somewhere with no crowds on the sidewalk. These houses all had yards, and lawns, and space. At the end of the street, right next to the hill, a two-story house sat, white sides and a white fence, dark blue trim surrounding the windows. It looked old—like Wild West old. I was glad that this part of the world didn't get big thunderstorms like we did in Chicago—the house looked like one good gust of wind could take it down.

"Don't tell me this is your house," I tried to keep the apprehension from my voice.

"The one and only."

I worried it would be a dump.

"We have it fixed up nice. Things around here aren't always how they appear," Aunt G told me, like she read my mind. "This used to be Sam's grandparent's house. They left it to her in their will, so we used the money we were planning for buying a house to fix up the inside. Next year, we're planning to work on the outside, but I have to say I kind of like the wild west look."

She was right—it was modern and beautiful inside, with brand new equipment in the kitchen. The bathrooms were spotless and contemporary; they even had a hot tub on a deck in the backyard, which Aunt G showed me how to use as she gave me a tour of the house. I had an enormous room all to myself, with a walk-in closet and ensuite bathroom.

"Wow, Aunt G! This is fantastic," I said.

"Be ready early," Aunt Gillian called up to me on her way out of the door an hour after we had arrived. "I'll drop you off at the visitor center before I go to bed in the morning."

With a smile and a wave, Aunt G went to work for the night. Since Aunt Sam was also on the night shift, but at the local hospital, I relaxed at home and let their cat get to know me. A few treats later, and she lay on the couch, letting me rub behind her ears while she purred.

After an hour of doing nothing, I decided I had better unpack. It didn't take long because I didn't have much to take with me. Pretty much all the clothes I had packed were new—courtesy of a shopping trip Mom had dragged me on.

"You need new clothes," she had said. "Your old ones aren't dressy enough for you to work in, and I am done seeing you in hoodies and sweatpants." I had lived in a hoodie and sweatpants while I had been sick. They were comfortable and warm and easy to take off without pulling out a chemo port. It was also easy to hide all the weight I had lost when I already wore baggy clothes.

"Come on, Mom," I had complained. "I don't need all this. My jeans and t-shirts will be okay."

"First of all, you need to have slacks and a button-down shirt for work. Second, what if you meet some famous scientists? Gillian might have dinner parties, and I want you to look good. You need to dress like you're an adult now. You can't embarrass your aunts in front of their friends and colleagues by looking like..." and on and on it went, until I relented.

Funnily enough, I was pretty sure it was Aunt Sam being a nurse that had finally convinced Mom to let me come and stay here. I can just imagine her thinking Sam would be a substitute mother for me, always checking up on my health like Mom did. But, I was positive that Aunt Sam would be cool and let me look after myself.

I sighed and looked out from my new bedroom window, which faced over the backyard and onto the hill. I knew the observatory was up on the hilltop, although I couldn't see it through all the trees.

I wasn't much into science. I mean, I knew the core concepts. Even though I struggled with math, it was interesting. I never got good grades in science, but I liked the classes. All the same, I figured it couldn't be too bad working for the observatory. I didn't know for sure what I would be doing. I imagined it would be telling people not to climb on telescopes, or not to touch things. I pictured myself standing around by myself a lot, monitoring stuff in a big indoor museum.

At least it wasn't a McJob, and, heck—I might even learn something. Still, it would be nice to get one or two days to chill and acclimate before I had to start; Aunt G had suggested that. Mom didn't want me to leave until right before my first day on the job. She had warned me about my expected behavior while staying with her sister. Not that I needed the lecture—I had always been a kind and polite person, or at least I tried to be. I saw no reason I would suddenly become a jackass in Flagstaff. I knew Mom didn't actually think I was likely to misbehave; it was just her first chance to be a normal mom again. Before I got sick, she would always nag. Now, she could nag and not worry that it might be the last thing she ever said to me. Is it weird that I appreciated the lectures and reprimands? They made me feel like life might start to go back to what it used to be.

As I started to get ready for bed, I looked in the bedroom mirror over the dresser into which I had emptied my suitcase. My red hair, green eyes, and the whiskers from the beard I was trying to grow stared back at me. I looked gaunt like I'd been very sick—which, of course, I had. A big scar ran down the center of my chest—signs of survival from my many surgeries. Another one ran down my left forearm, where they had taken some veins after a clot. I wanted to get a tattoo to cover it one day. I didn't find it ugly or anything—

I wanted the tattoo to be a mark of my surviving the cancer, something I could look at and feel good about.

Looking back in the mirror, I was glad to see one thing that hadn't changed: the decently sized bulge in my boxers. While impressive—if I did say so myself—I still sighed. I had barely grown into a man before the cancer had robbed me of my social life, and any chance I had to lose my virginity. And now that I was here, where nobody knew me, I felt my chances of losing it now were even slimmer.

With another sigh, I crawled into bed and waited to fall asleep. Luthien, the cat, jumped up onto my bed and lay down next to me. Her head rested in the crook of my arm; a paw draped lazily over my elbow. I stroked my hand through her long gray and white fur, and she purred and closed her eyes with a yawn.

I couldn't fall asleep. I tossed and turned a few times before I gave up and lay on my back. I stared at the ceiling, thinking of home and how I got here.

The day after my high school graduation ceremony, I had felt the first lump. It was under my arm—small, but noticeable. At first, I thought nothing of it, but then I found a lump under the other arm. Then, I tried very hard to stop noticing. By Halloween, I went to the doctor. They did tests and scans and more tests. But by Christmas, they told me for sure I had cancer. Lymphoma.

Mom wanted me to move back home, of course.

"Jeremy, you should come home so we can look after you," she had said.

"Mum, I only moved out a few months ago!" As part of the 'growing up experience,' Dad had talked Mom into the idea that I should move into the university residence. I couldn't get an apartment yet because I was only eighteen, and most places wouldn't rent to someone under twenty-one. Dad thought it would do me good to be on my own, away from home, but close enough that I could come back if something happened. Mom reckoned that cancer counted as that Something.

"Still, Jeremy..."

"Look, I'm only—what? Forty-five minutes away from home by train? And that's at rush hour."

"Jeremy, cancer is an enormous deal. You don't understand."

"Look," I had sighed, trying to keep my voice steady. "I appreciate that you want to look after me, but the doctors say some chemo and some radiation, and I will be okay. They say I will barely have to miss any school." Plus, I didn't want to give up my freedom after finally having discovered it —though that part I didn't say.

It's not that I didn't love my mom—I did. She was good and usually right. It's only that sometimes, she could also be a bit much to deal with—especially if something didn't go according to plan.

Well, as I said, she was right. I had to stop going to classes by spring break since my classmates didn't like that I threw up in class hourly. It didn't help that my brain seemed to be full of cotton, stopping synapses from firing. I had felt like a zombie who wasn't there, floating through each day. I was lucky that my professors were understanding; most sent copies of their lectures and homework. I could limp through the rest of the semester until the summer.

Once my lease was up, I ended up moving back home. I spent the summer alternating between lying in my childhood bed, a hospital bed, and the couch. I had hoped I would meet a girl during my first year and have something happen. I had been shy throughout high school and, like most teenagers, had taken the change to university to reinvent myself. I had been more outgoing until the cancer. I mean yeah, I wanted to lose my virginity, like most guys my age. But more than that, what I wanted was to be in love.

I kept getting sicker. Mom didn't want me to continue with school until I got better; I wanted to keep going. My dad, ever the peacemaker, brokered a compromise—I would do online courses. My program manager was understanding and waved some mandatory courses, pushing them to the next year. It was just enough credits so that I didn't lose the year.

The twins, eleven at the time, grew tired of me hogging the couch and getting all the attention. I told them to could fuck off and die with my cancer if they wanted—that had shut them up, but landed me in a serious load of shit with my parents.

"Jeremy, you being sick doesn't give you permission to swear in my house, especially at your sisters," Mom had raged.

Dad was more laid back—disappointed rather than angry.

"Jeremy, when you lash out like that at your sisters, you're teaching them that yelling and swearing are acceptable.

Instead, you could help them understand your illness and how they can help you. You're their big brother; they look up to you. I expect you to be a better role model," he had said.

"The girls are too young to understand what's happening to you. They only know that you're in their space and controlling many things this family does. They don't see how your medical treatment forces these things to happen; they only see you getting all this special attention. To them, being sick means you have a cold. They think you should be better by now."

That's my dad for you. I tried to keep my mood in check, and I lost it more times than I am proud of. Dying of cancer, and the drugs used to stop it from killing you quickly by killing you slowly instead will do that to you.

It got hard to tell which was which. One day, I started to bleed. From everywhere. Was that the cancer or the drugs? I lost my appetite. Cancer or drugs? I began to cough. Then I coughed so much I threw up. The muscles in my chest and my ribs seared with a pain so sharp it felt like I was being stabbed with hot knives. Place your bets, ladies and gentlemen... cancer or drugs?

I had tried therapy and support groups for my mental well-being during cancer treatment. They helped me to control my emotions better, even though I felt sicker and sicker every day.

I had begun to look like a skeleton with no hair, skinny as all get out, and sunken eyes and cheeks. I wondered if I would actually die. The doctors had told me the cancer was curable, but I seemed to be the big exception. Chemo usually works as a cure—except for with me. Radiation will shrink the tumors—except on me. I was glad I was doing the fall semester of second year online, and I didn't have to go out in public. I could just imagine women fainting, puppies howling, and cats hissing at the sight of me, men crying out 'good lord, what is that *thing?!*' as I walked by. It was much nicer just to stay home. I could go to school without leaving my bed.

Finally, the doctors said they needed to do something more radical—surgery to remove the tumors followed by intense chemo and radiation therapy. Even though I had just turned nineteen, I felt I had very little to do with the health decisions made for me. I just nodded and went along with it—a force of habit, I guess. I found it hilarious that my surgery was scheduled for Halloween.

The surgery was when I hit rock bottom. I was glad I was unconscious for it. They said I died twice on the table. As they removed the tumors, I guess they nicked the spleen, and it burst. I bled a lot. While they fixed that, somehow, the blood supply to my liver had become blocked with blood clots. They pulled veins from my arms to rebuild the blood supply to my liver and pancreas. I guess that's when my luck turned around. With most of the cancer gone, suddenly, the chemo worked. It was a miracle, according to Mom.

By spring break of my second year, I finally showed up with no evidence of cancer on my PET scan. They did another one three weeks later; same result. I had finished the first semester of second year through some miracle given that I had missed assignments, thanks to the surgery. Again, thank goodness for understanding professors and departments.

Mom got it into her head that I should take the rest of the semester off and get out of the city. She browbeat the doctors into agreeing that it would be best for me to get some sun and take things easy until summer. I could still enroll in the first semester of school for third year if I wanted, as long as I did some summer school. Mom had even arranged for me to go live with her younger sister. I was kind of surprised she would let me out of her sight until I remembered Aunt Sam being a nurse. Then it all fell into place.

I was angry this was all arranged without my knowing, but in the back of my mind, it relieved me. I had pushed myself too hard for that first term, even though I only took online courses. It was too much—I wanted a break. I still wanted and planned to take third year as scheduled. I would try to do some courses over the summer to finish second year. I loved my program, and I loved school. When most people my age would have used any excuse not to have to go to school so they could sit and play video games all day, I was once again the big exception. My mom put her foot down, and I got on the plane to Phoenix.

The twins were ecstatic I was going away; they would finally get the attention they had been craving for the last year and a half.

And now I was here, lying in a strange bed halfway across the country, too tired to sleep.

After a few more minutes, I sighed and opened my backpack, pulling out a vial of melatonin supplements I sometimes used to help me fall asleep. About five minutes after taking it, I drifted off.

I woke with a start to the alarm on my phone blaring. I forced my eyes open to see that it was six in the morning. With a groan, I stumbled to the shower, shaved, and put on some clothes. I had finished breakfast and started washing the dishes when Aunt Gillian pulled into the driveway.

"Well, look at you," she said with a smile. "Awake and everything. Almost like a responsible adult instead of a nineteen-year-old who should—by rights—still not have gone to bed yet."

"Not everyone is a night owl like you, GillyBean," my Aunt Sam said, following in through the door. Aunt G turned and smiled at her wife before leaning into the tall, thin woman for a quick peck on the lips. As a trauma nurse, Aunt Sam had worked the night shift at the hospital.

The smile on both their faces as they kissed showed how much in love they were. They expected me to be grossed out by love, so I played the part and made retching sounds. My aunts looked over at me and laughed. I gave Sam a hug.

"So unconvincing," Sam snorted while she laughed, her amber eyes crinkling.

"He's jealous, I'm sure," Aunt G replied, kissing Sam again and brushing her long raven hair. "Ready to go, Kiddo?"

"I'm not a kid," I muttered. "You're barely ten years older than me, anyway."

"More like fifteen. But I've got my doctorate, and now I'm a 'responsible adult,'" she replied. "All right, get in the car before I'm too tired to drive."

"A first—a woman who doesn't want to pretend to be younger than she is," Aunt Sam chimed in as she climbed the stairs, dropping her bag on the stand by the door.

"Yeah, yeah, call the newspaper," Aunt G called back, a smile across her face. She turned to me, "Alright, let's get out of here."

The ride up Mars Hill was winding and disorienting in the dark. The tall trees blocked whatever light the sun made so early in the morning. The dim streetlights seemed to make no difference to the gloom. The road twisted and turned as we climbed the hill. I didn't know why the streetlights out here were so dim, but I was too tired to ask. I felt like I yawned every twenty seconds as we drove.

"I hope you like the people you'll be working with. Beth runs the place. Kind of like a middle-aged grandmother. She wants everyone to be happy, but she also has an eye for detail and will be quick to let you know if you're out of line. Don't cross her, and you'll be okay. Her family's been out here pretty much forever. Most live out on the reservation up to the north. I think they own some land out near there, too.

"Who else should you know? There's Rebecca, one of my grad students, but she works at the visitor center as a tour guide when she doesn't have telescope time. She's incredibly smart and writes papers well. She only has to finish a bit more research to complete her thesis, but her drafts so far are very promising. Alice is another grad student, but she's not mine, so I don't know much about what she's working on. I only take one student a year so I can work on my research—publish or perish, after all."

I was only listening somewhat, letting my aunt talk like this meant I could take in the surroundings a little, trying to ready myself for the day.

"Let's see, who else do you need to know?" Aunt G continued. "There's Jim—he does a lot of the maintenance and has been there for ages, must be in his 70s now, but he sure doesn't act it. Nancy, his wife, runs the gift shop. Retirement job for her, she used to be the librarian at the university. You'll work mostly with Rebecca and Jim, I expect. They want you to take over tour duties when she gets back on the telescope in a couple of months. You can give Jim a hand with some maintenance work, too. All grad students get their telescope time from May to mid-August."

"Why does she get time during the summer?" I interjected. "Isn't that when the telescope would be most popular? I mean, that's gotta be the best season to be in Flagstaff, so people would want to come here then, no?"

"Actually, the summer can be the worst. The nights are short, so you can only see for a few hours before the sun comes up and it gets too bright. That's why the grad students get the time—no one else wants it. It's a busy time for them because it's also tourist season. Most work hospitality jobs in town or out at the Canyon as well as studying."

"Hmm, yeah, I guess that makes sense. Still, though, at least it's warm out."

"You know we work in a heated control room, right?" my aunt said with a laugh. She pulled into the parking lot at the summit of Mars Hill, stopping at the steps that lead up to the door of the dark building.

She wished me a good night—from her point of view anyway—and said that someone should come by and start opening up in the next half hour. I was glad I had brought my book to read and a thermos of tea to drink while I sat on the steps and waited. I could smell the pine trees through the breeze that made the branches shake ever so gently. The moon appeared over the top of the tallest tree, and below it, the glow of the sun followed its path, starting to light up the sky.

I was starting to get cold, despite the tea, when I heard a car driving through the trees. Soon, headlights pierced the dawn, and a maroon SUV pulled into the staff parking section. A portly Native American woman in her late 40s or early 50s jumped out of the car with more alacrity than her size would have let on. She bounded up the stairs and gave me an enormous grin.

"Jeremy!" she almost shouted. "I've been so looking forward to meeting you. I'm Beth. Your aunts and I are excellent friends. I've heard so much about you! Come in, come in!"

Before I even put my book in my backpack, she already had the door unlocked and held it open with a smile. Beth spoke a mile a minute and wasted no time in showing me around.

The center seemed to consist of two sizeable rooms on either side of the main hall, and a gift shop. Beth pointed to the hall on the right as we walked in. "That's the exhibit hall. We have exhibits in there for all ages, and sometimes we get touring exhibits in there too." She pointed to the other room on the left. "That's the cinema. We show movies about astronomy and the observatory in there every hour."

We arrived in the middle of the hall at the information and admissions booth.

The chief attraction, the grounds and telescopes, were through another door straight across from the entrance. Beth pointed it out, setting her bag down behind the information booth.

"You're the junior guy on the staff, so you're in charge of cleaning the men's room," she explained. She pointed at the bathrooms next to the booth. "But your number one priority will be to take over the tours so that Rebecca can have time to work on her thesis. She said she would be here early today. She wants to give you a quick overview of the grounds on the Mars Hill campus before you shadow her for the public tours." She gestured through the door and out toward the top of the hill again. "Oh, and I almost forgot—these are for you."

I took the red shirt and fleece she handed me, as well as a red windbreaker embossed with the Lowell Observatory logo—my name stitched below it. I changed in the washroom and stepped out in time to see another woman enter the lobby.

My heart skipped a beat—or you could say it stopped entirely for about five seconds. She was the most beautiful woman I had ever seen. She maybe came up to my shoulder. Brown hair tied back in a ponytail. Milk chocolate eyes. Pale complexion, but with rosy cheeks sprinkled with freckles, and a pixie-like body. I don't know how I knew, but right then, I knew my life that had changed forever—I hoped, for the better. I gasped—I had forgotten to breathe.

"Rebecca! How was your weekend?" Beth asked with the hint of a smile pulling at her lips.

"Good, Beth. Got a bit of sleep, but I've been working so much I barely know what a day off feels like. So," she turned to me, "you're the new guy, are you?" She had a faint accent I recognized but couldn't place, and a voice that sounded like wooden wind chimes—full of melody.

"I'm... uh..." I stammered.

"Rebecca, this is Jeremy," Beth answered for me. "He's Gillian's nephew."

Rebecca extended her hand. "Nice to meet you."

"Yeah... Yeah... You, too," I said, reaching out to shake it. *Come on, Jeremy—pull yourself together,* I thought.

When our hands touched for the first time, there were actual physical sparks.

"Ow!" she said, snapping her hand away, laughing. "You shocked me!"

Beth shook her head. "It must be the fleece."

"I am so sorry, Rebecca." I apologized. Her skin had been so soft. She reached out again, handshake firm and steady, confident.

"Don't worry about it," Rebecca shrugged. "The air is dry here, so you'll find you build up more static than normal. So, you're the infamous nephew from Chicago, huh?"

"Well, I don't know about infamous. I mean, I'm a nice guy, but I haven't really done anything... I guess that's me, though," I stammered, mortified at my seeming inability to speak a coherent sentence in front of Rebecca.

Rebecca grinned. Did she find amusement in my discomfort?

"Oh, come on, Rebecca, can't you see the poor boy is jet-lagged?" Beth poured tea she had been making in the staff room into three mugs and handed them to us. "No wonder he can't seem to think straight. You only got an hour of sleep last night, didn't you? You're jet-lagged like mad, aren't you, dear?"

I smiled and took a sip of the hot tea. It seemed to clear my head and stopped me from acting more stupid than I already had. I liked Beth—she reminded me a lot of my mother and Aunt G. But Rebecca? Well, she was something else entirely.

With introductions out of the way, Beth sent Rebecca and me out to walk the grounds while she opened the museum for the first visitors. Rebecca gave me a quick tour of the highlights of the Mars Hill grounds. She showed me the Clark telescope, which was one of the biggest refractor telescopes in the world. She also led me to the tomb of Percival Lowell, the founder buried on the grounds of his observatory.

"Lowell set up an observatory here because it was the middle of nowhere. He bought the Clark telescope and had it shipped here piece by piece. Mars obsessed him—he thought there was life on it, which is why he called this place Mars Hill. And when I tell you it obsessed him, I really mean it. He thought he could see canals and cities. He sketched them all and named them. We have some of his sketches over in the library," Rebecca explained as we walked through the grounds. She pointed out a sizeable building with a round dome that I had thought was some sort of planetarium.

"Turns out it was all in his head—possibly literally. Some researchers suggested that what he saw might have been internal structures in his eye. They could have reflected into the telescope optics, so they looked like they were on the planet."

Finally, she took me to the telescope that had discovered Pluto—the actual telescope. It had displeased Lowell Observatory when their most famous discovery, Pluto, was demoted to a dwarf planet several years earlier. The observatory had several displays devoted to making the case that it was still an extraordinary discovery.

When I was sixteen, my dad took me with him on a business trip to Washington, DC. I had wandered around the mall while he worked. The first thing I did was go to the war memorials I had seen in movies. Standing there in real life, reading the names of everyone who had died, was a haunting experience. I wasn't expecting it to be so impactful. I had drifted up the steps to the Lincoln Monument. I read the words of hope and emancipation etched on the inside of the building. I had just been leaving down the steps when something caught my eye—one stone on the steps marked the place where Martin Luther King made his 'I have a dream' speech. I found myself tearing up at the history of the place.

Now, walking into the dome and seeing the telescope that had discovered 'America's Planet' evoked similar feelings. I was glad I didn't start weeping this time. The telescope was smaller than I had thought—nowhere near as impressive as the Clark telescope had been. The whole thing was also painted an odd salmon-pink color.

"What's with the boxing mitt on the balancing arm?" I asked. I pointed at the glove attached to a pole at head height that held counterweights to keep the telescope balanced and easy to move.

"I knew it!" she said, hitting my shoulder with a laugh. She led me back down the stairs in the dome to the ground floor entrance. "I knew you were holding back on me."

"Well, you can't have an astronomer for an aunt and not pick up some stuff about astronomy," I said.

"The boxing glove is to stop you from smashing your brains out if you hit your head on the arm at night. Anyway, this is where the tour ends, but we still have some time. Let's hide here, so Beth doesn't find something for us to do," Rebecca smiled and closed the door to the telescope.

I raised my eyebrows to her before darkness filled the room.

"That way, no one will stumble in here and catch us slacking off." There was a soft click. Red lights that astronomers used when making observations came on, allowing us to still see. "So, tell me more about you, Jeremy."

"Well, I'm not that interesting."

"I'll be the judge of that," she said with a smile and an expectant look.

All at once, my stomach filled with butterflies, and my hands moistened.

"Well..." I began. "I grew up in Chicago and made it through high school, somehow. I'm studying for a BA in history and a minor in music. I had some health problems, so everyone thought it would be a good idea for me to get out of the city for a while. Aunt Gillian offered to take me in. She found me this job to keep me busy while I get better. I'm going back for my third year in the fall."

"What part of history are you studying?" I looked up, surprised that her first question wasn't about my health. Usually, if you tell people you have health problems, the first thing they want to know is what kind—like somehow, you might make them sick, too.

"One of my professors has a hard-on for how languages shaped history. I'm a bit of a nerd if you haven't noticed. I am investigating the international language, Esperanto."

"Esperanto?" she asked. Her eyes locked onto mine—I felt like I could swim in the rich chocolate color. She smiled, and I snapped back to my senses, answering her question. At least I had remembered to keep breathing this time. If I wasn't careful, my relationship with her—whatever that was—might be hazardous to my health.

"Yeah, it's this auxiliary language invented so that it's easy to learn."

"I know, I've heard of it. They used to write scientific papers in it for a while. It would be a lingua franca for the science community."

Now I was surprised again; few people knew about Esperanto.

"I studied science history," she said, reading my surprise. "So, why the focus on that language over any other?"

"Well, when I was in grade ten, I read this book called *Off to be the Wizard* by Scott Meyer. It's about these geeks who discover a file that proves the universe is a simulation. Almost immediately, they get caught doing strange things. One makes his car run forever without needing gas. Another deposits a load of money in his bank accounts— stuff like that. One by one, they all escape to Medieval England and live as wizards. They use Esperanto as a kind of magic language to control their computer scripts. It's a very fun book. I had never heard of Esperanto before then, so I did some research on it and lived my life. I only started rereading the book when I had time off during the summer before first year.

"This time, it inspired me to learn the language, especially since it's easy on the web or Duolingo now. It was hard to learn, despite its reputation for being easy. I almost gave up until I started having to go to the doctor a lot. The thing that kept inspiring me was that the name 'Esperanto' comes from its own word for hope. I needed some hope then, so I became active in the Esperanto community. I had a lot of time to be on my phone working on learning the language. I could also take part in online community events in Esperanto. And the more I learned about it, the more I could think about something that didn't involve cancer. When I had to pick a project to work on for my undergrad thesis, you could say the choice was obvious."

I looked up at her, expecting to see boredom or some lack of understanding, but what I got was a full smile. I got the sense that my story was close to something that she had experienced herself.

"What is it that draws you to history? It's obvious you have a passion for words and language. Why not linguistics or philology?" Rebecca asked, raising one of the most graceful eyebrows I had ever seen.

"You know about philology?" She impressed me. Few people who didn't study languages even knew the term—the actual study of language, including structure, history, and relationships to other languages.

"Tolkien fan. You can't appreciate his work without appreciating his love of the languages he invented," she said.

I stared; Rebecca was full of surprises.

"So... history?" she prompted.

"Oh, right. I like history because it lets me look at the past and compare and contrast it with today. To use where we were and are now to look into the future. I mean, it's not fortune-telling, but noting cycles in climate, economics, and politics to use them as factors for prediction is common—so why not language? One day, we may need an international language again. It's important to know why it failed and what could have made the language more successful."

"I guess I can see that," Rebecca nodded. "What kind of music are you interested in?" she asked, abruptly changing the topic.

"All kinds, but I used to study classical voice," I said, smiling at her tactic to keep me on my conversational toes.

"Oh, a singer—that's cool. I'll get you to sing something for me one day."

"How about you?"

"Well, I'm not much for music these days, but I used to play keyboard. Sometimes I get together with friends; we pretend to be in a metal band and do cover songs. I play drums with them. I'm good at keeping rhythm."

"Cool, but that's not what I meant. I mean, what's your past? Where are you from? How did you end up here?"

She grinned. "Doing some historical research?"

"Purely professional interest," I replied with a wink. I shocked myself. Was I flirting? Was this... flirting? It couldn't be, right? I had barely been able to speak to her half an hour ago. I wasn't usually this talkative to strangers, much less to women as pretty as Rebecca. She was easy to talk to.

"Well, I'm from Kings Canyon in Australia and grew up in the Outback. It's a beautiful place with a lot of stars. When I was little, I wanted to know what they were, so my mum took me down to the library the next time we went to Alice Springs, and I asked for a book on stars. The librarian gave me one full of people like Hugo Weaving and Peter Allen."

I couldn't help but chuckle at the misunderstanding. She beamed at me, eyes twinkling with a bit of mischief.

"I had to explain it wasn't the book I wanted, not at all. Eventually, we figured it out. When I turned ten, my dad gave me my first telescope." Had I imagined a slight hitch in her voice when she said 'dad'? "Once I had done my undergrad studies, I got accepted right away to do grad work at

Melbourne University and doctoral work here with your Aunt. I've been in the states two years now."

"I have to ask, and I know it's rude, so forgive me—but aren't you a bit young to be going for a PhD?"

"I'm twenty-five—I got into university a bit early and studied through summers. Luckily, my family could afford for me not to work, so I shaved off a few years and just did really well," she said, blushing. "Sorry, don't mean to brag. How old are you?"

"Nineteen. I turn twenty in August," I answered, worried that she might think I was too young. "What are you working on with Aunt G?"

"Exoplanets. You know—planets that orbit stars that aren't our own?"

I nodded at her.

"Right, figured you would," she said, nodding. "I'm trying to refine the ways we can detect them here on earth. I have a paper to present in six weeks that I'm reviewing with Dr. Gillian. I need to finish my data collection so I can finish my thesis." She drew a bit closer and looked me right in the eye. Her eyes were deep and beautiful, like an ocean of brown waves flecked with green and blue whitecaps.

Heat rushed through my body.

"You know," she whispered, "I feel like I've known you for ages. I'm not normally this talkative, but it feels like we've been friends forever. You're easy to talk to."

"I feel the same way." I gulped, surprised and gratified to hear my own thoughts from earlier come back at me. Maybe I felt like we were a lot more than just friends.

She stood toe-to-toe now and tilted her face up at me. Did she want me to kiss her? My body went into panic mode—I'd only known her a few hours. Yeah, we were getting along well, but this was fast...

"God damn, you're tall," she muttered. With a wicked laugh, she pinched me on the arm and threw open the door. I was both disappointed and relieved.

The morning was a blur of learning what to do for the tour. And, to my shock, flirting with Rebecca. Before I knew it, the day was over.

"You two seem to get on okay," Beth observed as we completed our final cleanup for the evening. According to Rebecca, most nights held activities at the observatory, which reopened much later in the evening, but tonight was one of the rare ones they had off.

"He's okay, I guess. For an undergrad," Rebecca teased.

"All that I ask that you keep it professional in the workplace." Beth gave her a sharp, knowing look. I darted a look at Rebecca and saw her glance at me too before quickly turning back to Beth, whose glare slowly turned to a smile. "You two would be a cute couple. But what do I know? I'm just an old woman who works here."

Rebecca and I exchanged a look.

"You don't have to worry, ma'am," I said, feeling my cheeks heat up. "We're just friends. I mean, we just met today..."

"Enough with that 'ma'am' talk, Jeremy. And sure—you tell yourself that if you want. If I want fiction, I'll watch reality TV. Speaking of which..." Beth glanced down at her watch. "Looks like it's time for me to get home. Survivor is starting, and it's so rare to have a night off. Make sure you lock up everything, Rebecca."

Beth was halfway to her SUV by the time she had finished talking. We waved as she drove out of the parking lot.

"Alone, at last," Rebecca sighed. She, too, looked at her watch and said, "I have to go. Got plans tonight."

"Boyfriend?" I asked with a stab of jealousy. My stomach felt like it was deflating at the thought. Disgust immediately followed the jealousy—of course she would have a boyfriend, and what right did I have to feel upset or jealous about it?

"Ha. No—don't have one of those," she said with a laugh. I felt an enormous wave of relief, despite myself. "I'm having dinner with my sister. She got into the university here for next year. We're going to eat then look at apartments so we can live together and save some money. She flew up for a visit and a house-hunting trip. She probably just woke up, actually—the jetlag has been really hard on her." She looked at me pensively and then, as she finished locking the door and setting the alarm, said, "I'm not working tomorrow, which means you aren't either until you're trained. Want to meet up tonight after dinner? My sister Abby will want to explore the college nightlife on her own, I suspect. I have something to show you that you might find cool if you're up for it."

"Um, yeah, that would be great. Um, I don't have a car or anything..." I felt embarrassed to suddenly be acting like the weak-kneed and stammering Jeremy of this morning. I made a mental note to buy a vehicle, so I didn't have to keep relying on my aunt for a ride everywhere.

"No problem. I'll pick you up at Dr. Gillian's house—I know where it is, we meet up there sometimes to talk about my thesis. Does ten o'clock work?"

"Um, yeah."

"Great—see you then." Rebecca jumped into her car and drove away, leaving me staring at the empty parking lot.

2

"How was your day, Jer?" Aunt Sam asked when she picked me up from the empty parking lot in front of the interpretive center a few minutes later.

"It was good." I enjoyed the view as we pulled out of the parking lot. Flagstaff opened up below us before we started the windy road down the hill.

"Make any new friends?"

"Well, yeah. Beth is great! Hilarious, and still maternal."

Aunt Sam laughed, navigating the many turns that brought us down from the top of the hill and into the valley that housed Flagstaff.

"As if being maternal and hilarious are mutually exclusive," she said, turning to look at me. "Spill it, Jer, what else happened?"

"I met this girl..."

"I knew it. Better tell me details, mister," she laughed.

"She's beautiful. Kind, funny, and just... exceptional. I don't really have the words..." I stammered, my infatuation with Rebecca getting me tongue-tied... again. Thinking about her sent adrenaline into my veins and butterflies into my stomach. "I haven't felt like this about someone in a very, very long time. No—I take that back."

"Oh?" my aunt said with a glint of worry in her green eyes as she shot me a look.

"Hey!" I exclaimed. "Eyes on the road! But yeah, I do take it back. I've never felt this way about anyone before—ever."

"Sounds like an enjoyable day, then," my aunt said with a smile. "Gillian and I want you to fit in and enjoy yourself out here, Jer. I'm glad that you're..." she looked at me sideways, "making friends."

"Eyes on the road!"

She winked at me.

"She asked me to meet up with her tonight," I blurted out.

"Oh, she did now? And what is this lucky girl's name?"

"Rebecca."

"The same Becca that's Gillian's student?" she asked carefully.

"Yes. Why?" The change in Aunt Sam's voice surprised me.

"Just... Be kind to her, Jer. She's had darkness in her past. She's a sweet girl, of course—kind and generous. But don't think you can play with her and then drop her. She's had a rough life."

This news surprised me. The picture she had given me of her life in Australia and her family didn't seem rough to me. Was she lying when she told me about her home? Or was my aunt being paranoid? I was also a little insulted. I wasn't the kind of person who would play with someone's emotions maliciously.

"I wouldn't," I said, hurt.

Aunt Sam sighed.

"I know. I'm glad she's opening up with you, she's been so reserved since she's been here. No dates, hardly any non-work friends that Gillian or I know of. I'm glad she picked you to be friends with. You have a good heart."

Now I really didn't know what to think.

With that, we pulled into the driveway. I took a nap because I was still jetlagged, and I had some time to kill. My dreams were black and void of color, with Rebecca screaming at me for rescue and then falling into darkness. I woke up with a start at eight to Aunt Gillian shaking my foot to get me up for dinner. I ate and then took a shower. By the time ten o'clock rolled around, I was ready to go.

I sat in the living room playing with a laser, Luthien chasing it around the room. I kept stealing glances at the gloomy street, looking for some sign of Rebecca.

After what felt like an hour, she pulled into the driveway—ten o'clock on the dot.

"See you later!" I called out to my aunts, bounding down the steps and toward the driveway.

"Don't stay out too late!" Aunt Gillian called from where she stood in the doorway, an arm draped around Sam's shoulders.

"See you!" I called back, trying not to sound like a teenager going on his first 'date' while I got into Rebecca's car. The entire scene was so stereotypical that it almost made me laugh now that the waiting was over.

"Hey, Jeremy," Rebecca said, peeling out the driveway.

"What's the rush?" The jerky motions threw me back into my seat as I struggled to buckle my seatbelt.

"Oh, I just have a surprise for you."

We drove for a few minutes before I recognized where we were heading. "I thought the observatory was closed for the night?"

"It is," she said; then she became silent for a while longer.

I wondered what was going on. Before we made the last turn to the observatory, she pulled left into a lookout I hadn't noticed earlier that day. Rebecca stopped the car. I looked over at her and saw she wore a snug blue tank top that, in profile, highlighted her breasts. They were small and looked like they would be a perfect fit in my hand. I was hard in an instant, much to my embarrassment.

"Checking out the view?" she asked, raising one eyebrow when she caught me staring.

A flush of embarrassment at being caught rushed to my face.

"Come on." She pulled on a hoodie and nodded for me to get out of the car. I thought I saw her lips pull into a smile in her reflection in the car's window before the inside lights turned off.

The mild temperature surprised me. I could smell spring in the air, although there some snow still lay on the ground. We walked over to a stone wall in front of her car's bumper and looked out over the city.

"Why is it so dark?" I blurted. I was used to the lights of Chicago, where you could easily read, walk, or even conduct minor surgery under the ultra-bright LED streetlights.

She laughed softly. "Figured you would notice. And call me Becca—Rebecca is so formal. It's so the city doesn't interfere with the observatories. There are a few big ones in town, not only Lowell. They have a bylaw that regulates streetlight brightness, direction, and color. It makes for some wonderful night skies. Look at Orion there. It's easy to see the nebula in his junk." She turned and grinned at me.

"What?" I said with a laugh, heat rising on my cheeks. I knew the constellation, but had no idea about any 'junk.'

"Well, it's supposed to be a sword, but who wears their sword in the middle of their belt in front of their body? We all know it's actually Orion's dick," she said, lightly laughing at the joke.

I could see a blue cloud surrounding one star on the... sword. "It's cool," I stammered, her explicit language taking me by surprise.

A van pulled into the lookout beside us. Two teenagers jumped from the driver and passenger side doors, then hopped in the back. Within minutes, the windows on their car fogged over.

"Did you bring me to the local make-out spot?" I asked, a little too hopeful.

"It's a lookout, Jeremy," Rebecca said with mild exasperation. "It has lots of purposes. But right now, look out...at the sky." She leaned back and lay over the hood of her car. Seeing her laid out like that showed how petite she was. And I could imagine no one more attractive.

I followed suit, and we both stared into the depths of space, laying across the hood. Then we talked. Before I knew it, it was past midnight. We had spent the last ten minutes lying in silence. The teens had long since had their fun and gone, leaving us to our quiet contemplation of the stars. The wind rustled the trees. Above us, Orion had passed from view over our heads.

"Do you believe in God?" she asked, breaking the quiet.

"No," I answered. I didn't know why she asked and hoped I had given the right answer. "Do you?"

"No. I grew up Jewish, but you can't study the universe and still believe. At least, I couldn't."

"I grew up Catholic; I even sang in the choir. I don't think I ever actually believed in it, though—not really."

And with that, we descended once more into silence. I turned my head to look at her and could see a slight smile across her lips, her eyes only half-open. A few minutes later, we also left the lookout. We drove in silence back down Mars Hill to my Aunt's house. It wasn't an awkward silence, though—it felt comfortable.

Becca got out of her car when we got to Aunt G's. We didn't kiss, but we hugged. The feeling of her body touching mine was amazing. She was soft and warm. Firm yet tender. Ripples of lust spread through my body. Afterward, as I lay in bed, I remembered her warmth. I was still not sure exactly what kind of relationship we had, if any. Was there a chance for us to be more than colleagues? And if there was, how much more? Thoughts raced through my head, and I tossed and turned but couldn't sleep.

You're being stupid, I thought to myself. *You met this morning for Bob's sake. Try to relax and see where this goes. Neither of you owes anything more to each other than being coworkers. If something else develops, then great—but take it easy.*

I dozed off and had another dream about Becca. She was running in panic and asked me to help her escape, but everywhere I turned, there was nothing but sand. She sank into the red earth, reaching up to me with tracks of red sand sticking to her tear-moistened cheeks. She was up to her waist, then her shoulders, then her chin. She struggled, one arm above her head as the sand closed over her, eyes wide with panic. I pulled on her hand, but it ripped from me as I struggled to hold on, watching it also sink beneath the ground.

The next few weeks went by in what seemed like a flash. Becca taught me the ropes of giving tours. Within a week, I was doing the tours myself, with her following along and making sure I didn't screw up.

I also started working at night when the observatory reopened for public viewing. It was surprising how popular the event was for both tourists and locals. We had several smaller telescopes on tripods that Becca showed me how to set up and align. I spent a few weeks helping with general tasks, like cleaning the men's room more times than I cared to count. Finally, I got my chance to cover an eight-inch telescope that pointed toward Jupiter.

That night I was nervous, but Becca coached me through what people would ask. She posed as a tourist, asking questions with her singsong voice.

"Does Jupiter have rings?" she asked.

"Yes."

"Can I see the giant red spot?"

"No, it's currently on the other side of the planet, but you can see its colorful bands."

"Are those its moons?"

"Yes, you can see four moons—one on the left side and three on the right."

"Very good," Becca said with a smile. "People usually have only three questions about Jupiter. Most of the time, they just think it's cool."

And she was right. That first night I had nothing to worry about. Lots of people said it was 'Cool' or 'Awesome,' and they all asked the same three questions. When the night was over, and Becca helped me to pack the telescopes away, she had a mischievous idea.

"So, I've told the people working the Clark telescope that we would put it to bed for them. You need to learn how to do it," she began.

I groaned at the extra work; I was tiring after being awake for so long.

"Since we're the ones locking up, we can do some observations through the telescope before we put it to bed. I have some cool stuff to show you—just promise you won't tell anyone. The telescope is over a hundred years old, and we aren't supposed to play with it," She turned to me with a grin.

So we did. We looked at Jupiter through the big old telescope. It was even cooler than looking at it through the eight-inch one I had worked with earlier.

Then we looked at Mars.

I remembered what Becca had said to me about Percival Lowell and his obsession with the red planet. And then I thought about the Apollo astronauts that had used the telescope to look for landing sites on the moon.

I looked again at the long tube that towered over us, and it felt like the universe came crashing down on me. It was like... I could trace a single line from the first telescopes made in Holland, through Galileo and Newton and Lowell to us here. Standing under this massive telescope under a thin slice of sky, surrounded by the red glow of the dome's insides. I had been growing more interested in the actual science of astronomy. Since I was a history major, I knew the history of science, but not what it all meant, not really. That was the first night the awesomeness of the universe struck me.

The next morning, I picked some flowers from Aunt Gillian's garden. Becca and I lay them at Lowell's tomb, which was steps away from the door to the Clark telescope dome. Becca presented me with my first astronomy book —*Astrophysics for People in a Hurry* by Neil deGrasse Tyson. I finished it that day, and then devoured his lectures on YouTube.

As the outside temperature rose, the tension between us kept climbing, too. Even though we snuck off all the time to talk in areas away from the observatory—often cleaning old equipment or sweeping forgotten paths to keep Beth happy —we never kissed. In fact, we did nothing more than an occasional brush of an arm or hand against each other while we worked. But the more we talked, the more thought I was falling in love with Becca. I mean, it had to be love, right? Thinking about her made me smile. My heart felt like it would burst. I had a warm feeling in my stomach that felt like a cross between nervousness and the warmth of having drunk a pot of tea. Whatever it was, it felt great—at least if I didn't think about the chance she might not feel the same way. If I focused on that, I felt like I was about to throw up.

My phone rang when I got home from work one day. I answered.

"Jeremy, why is it you never call me?" my mom said evenly.

"Hi, Mom, what's up?"

"Other than having a son who never thinks about me? Nothing," she said, her sarcasm evident.

It was a ritual we had, and I was used to the steps. She would call and nag me about not calling. I would apologize.

Then we would laugh and chat for a while. It seemed weird, but it was something we had always done when I was away.

"You never call me, either," I said, playing out the next part of the conversation.

"I just did."

"Sorry, Mom. What's up?"

"I want to hear about your life! Are you healthy? How is living with Gillian and Sam? Are you enjoying your work? Have you made any friends?"

"Um... Yes, good, yes, and yes," I said.

"What's her name?" Mom asked, to my surprise. I immediately knew I should have expected this.

"Aunt Gillian!" I called out. "What have you been telling my mom?"

"I haven't told my sister anything!" Aunt Gillian replied from the kitchen.

"It was me," Aunt Sam called from the living room.

"Aunt Sam! Come on..." I shouted, then I sighed. I turned back to the phone. "Her name is Becca, Mom. And she's just a friend."

"That's not what I heard. Tell me about her."

"She is one of Aunt G's students. She taught me how to do the tours. We're just friends, really. I wish there were more to tell, but really, that's it."

"So, does she like you back?"

"I don't know. I think so? I mean, I know she does as a friend, but I don't know about more than that."

"Hmm," Mom said. "How have you been feeling?"

"Less tired. I don't know if that's from being healthier, or the air, or what."

"Have you found a doctor to book you in for your next PET scan?"

"I haven't, but I will..."

"How are your panic attacks?" she asked.

Lymphoma fucks up your blood, right? And oxygen in your blood helps to keep your stress hormones under control. Well, I had an acute problem with anxiety and panic attacks. The first one, not surprisingly, was just after I got the diagnosis. My heart literally hurt. It felt like something in it had snapped. I couldn't stop my racing thoughts and my bodies' instinct to run away. I had learned, through the course of my treatment, how to handle these kinds of things. I could cope with them much better now, but they still sucked.

"Haven't had one since I got here."

"That's good. Are you doing the breathing exercises?"

"Yes. You don't need to nag me, Mom."

"I know—I just miss you. I can't wait for you to come home," she said.

"Yeah, me too," I said, but I wasn't sure I was telling the truth.

"Are you going to do those summer courses to catch up on your schooling?"

"Actually, I already am—I started them last week. The schedule at the observatory isn't really that hard, so I wrote to the university to sign up for online courses. I can't do a few of my program courses, but I can take care of electives online over the summer."

"I'm happy to hear that. Aunt Sam is keeping a good eye on you?" she asked.

"Well, I'm not in any trouble, if that's what you're asking. I'm happy and healthy. It's getting warmer, so I was thinking about starting to explore the area. It's pretty neat out here."

There was silence on the line.

"Mom, are you still there?"

"Yeah," she said. "Sorry. I was eating."

"Oh, crap! I totally forgot about dinner."

"Language, Jeremy...," Mom said disapprovingly.

"Sorry. I forgot I promised to make food for Aunt Sam and Aunt Gillian tonight. I have to run, or I'll be late. Later, Mom!"

"Okay, Jer. Talk to you later. Love you."

"Love you, too. Say hi to the girls for me," I said, and then hung up. I made a mental note to ask my aunts to stop sharing everything going on in my life with my mother.

Becca. She was haunting me. I pictured her in my mind's eye, and my heart skipped a beat at the thought. I stood smiling for a while, just thinking about her. Then I shook myself and started making food. Chorizo sausage. That sounded like a nice unhealthy but delicious meal. I got to work.

3

THE NEXT DAY was not a glorious one. Becca wasn't there—her telescope time had arrived. I'd been dreading that happening. Now I was on my own at work. Becca had trained me well, though, and I didn't have any trouble leading tours and answering questions. For two weeks, Becca worked vampire hours with my Aunt G.

I started going for walks around the neighborhood. The walking turned to jogging and then to running, as I acclimated to the high elevation in Flagstaff. My strength was coming back. I always listened to music as I ran, but I rarely concentrated on it, my mind preoccupied with Becca.

My only contact with her came from text messages.

Becca: So, how was your first day without me there to make sure you don't mess it up? ;)

Me: Oh, you know. I only made some important discoveries on the Clark that would put all professional astronomers to shame.

Becca: LOL nice. I miss being there.

Me: We miss you, too. How is telescope time going?

Becca: Fine.

I couldn't help but feel a sting in the one-word answer. I had tried to shrug it off—I knew she was busy. I also knew that she couldn't say too much about what she was working on. She had told me she had to sign non-disclosure agreements as part of her program. They wouldn't want another team of astronomers to know what they were working on and beat them to publication. So, I did what I could to look past it without letting it get me down.

Me: Well, that's good. Anyway, been a long day, worked the day shift, and then the night observation, so I'm pretty tired. Hope your night goes well. G'night.

Becca: Thanks. Sleep well.

The messages continued like that. I would get an occasional text from Becca asking how things had gone at the observatory and how things were going with me. When I asked how things were going with her at the telescope, though, I never got more than a one-word reply, so I stopped asking. I straightened my shoulders and knew that this would pass— I would see her again soon, so I carried on with my tours and waited for her return.

But two weeks came and went, and she didn't come back to work. I didn't see her again except for a brief wave every once in a while when she and my aunt carpooled. Finally, unable to bear the distance any longer, I asked my aunt what was going on.

"Something exciting for Becca," she said. "I hope it goes well for her. Let her have time, and I hope she will have wonderful news soon."

Me: Hey Becca. I know you're busy. Wish you were around more. A new shawarma place has opened up on Aspen street. Would love to treat you to dinner sometime when you're free.

Twenty-four hours later, I got my reply.

Becca: Dinner sounds lovely. I have already put it in my calendar for my first night free. I'm sorry I've been so out of touch. It's just been so much work. I'm barely doing anything except monitoring the telescope and writing up my findings. It will be over soon. I miss you.

I felt so relieved. It was like a weight I didn't know I was carrying had lifted.

Over the weeks I had been in Flagstaff, it had already begun to feel like home to me. I had borrowed Aunt Gillian's car a few times and checked out some of the surrounding area. I went hiking near Sedona, and I went to the Grand Canyon. I sent Becca a few pics of me out and about.

Becca: Looks like you're having fun.

Me: Yeah, I am. The Canyon is bigger than I ever expected. I've only ever seen it in cartoons and thought they were exaggerating, but boy was I wrong.

Becca: We should go sometime when schoolwork lets us have a few days off.

Me: Do you know when that will be?

Becca: For me, not for a while. I think. Dr. Gillian really has me working hard. I feel like my brain has turned to mush some days.

Me: Yeah, I think my brain has been stagnant for too long. Thanks for reminding me to get started on my courses, too.

Becca: No problem!

A few weeks later, I sat at the kitchen table one afternoon, working on some online courses. The thing I liked about them was that I could do them any time I wanted. I had already finished one of the four I had to do and was halfway done with the second, making excellent progress on it.

"Hey, Jeremy," Aunt Sam said, sitting across the table with a cup of coffee in her hand. "Are you doing schoolwork?"

"Hi, Aunt Sam. Yeah—I'm trying to get all these courses done so I can decide what I want to do for next year," I closed my laptop and set it aside. "How are you? Just got up? Do you want some breakfast?"

"No, no, I'm okay—Gillian and I are taking the night off, so we'll go out for breakfast and then have a little date night. Thank you, though."

"No worries," I said, using a term Becca had taught me.

"I wanted to ask you, though. Are you happy here?" Aunt Sam asked.

The question surprised me.

"Of course. I kind of never want to leave," I said with a laugh.

Aunt Sam smiled.

"I'm glad to hear that. Though, is it because you like living in Flagstaff, or is it because of Rebecca?"

I took a breath.

"Well," I said, "I can't say that Becca isn't a little part of why I enjoy living here, and I'm in no rush to go home. But I like Flagstaff. I love living with you and Aunt Gillian. It feels less like you're looking out for me and more like we're just friends living together. I like how old-timey this town is, and I like small-town living. I thought I would find it weird not being surrounded by people, but it's something I can sure get used to."

"We like you living with us, too. I just wanted to make sure you know if, and why, you want to stay," Aunt Sam said, pulling out a small card from her wallet. "This is the Dean of the history department at Northern Arizona University. She's an old friend of a friend. I told her you might be interested in transferring, and she said if you are, to call her."

"Wow. Thanks, Aunt Sam," I said. "That's really great. I'll think about it."

"Do, Jeremy. You're welcome to stay here with us, but I want you to think about what you want. Just remember that it's silly to decide because of love if you don't know how she feels."

The next Monday, on the late shift, Beth cornered me.

"Hi, Jeremy, I have a task for you."

"Hey, Beth, What's up?"

"I need you to pack up one of the eight-inch telescopes we use for our observation nights. You and I are going up to the reservation to be the Lowell outreach staff for an event with the Hopi and Navajo peoples. We will be up there late, so I'm giving you the morning off tomorrow so you can sleep in. We usually have a little get together around the solstice. You know that's in a few days, right?"

"Of course. How late are we going to be?" I asked, thinking I had better let my aunts know I would be home late.

"Oh, I expect four or five am, once we get back and unpacked. And don't worry—I already told Gillian I would snag you for this, so she knows you'll be out late."

"Okay, sounds good, Beth," I said with a grin. I ran up the hill to grab one of the telescopes and some educational material Beth had asked for.

We packed up everything in Beth's SUV. The enormous barrel of the telescope lay across the back seats with the rest of the hardware and literature in the trunk. I had grown used to telescopes by now. Before I started working at the observatory, I thought telescopes were delicate things, and that they needed to be kept very still and protected. That is true of the big research telescopes. I had learned, though, that most portable scopes could deal with some handling. In fact, most of the amateur astronomers buckled their telescopes into their cars or laid them across their back seats. I had seen them unpacking in the parking lot one day and asked them about it. They told me that protective cases are only used if you're traveling by air or taking a super-lengthy trip. Becca had taught me how to line up the telescope with a simple tool and a screwdriver. Once done, the telescope was good as new, so you could travel and then realign it, even after a long road trip.

I jumped in the front as Beth climbed into the driver's seat and started the engine. We made our way down the hill and out of Flagstaff.

Beth asked me lots of questions about life in Chicago, like what it was like growing up there, about the twins and my parents, and my favorite books and movies. She also asked about university, my program, and what I hoped to do with it. I told her about my interest in Esperanto, and, of course, I told her about my cancer.

When most people find out I almost died from cancer, they usually become uncomfortable and change the subject; it's like having cancer makes you unspeakable. Not Beth, though. She asked me methodical questions about the diagnosis, what my treatment had been, and what my prognosis was.

It was cathartic to talk about it.

As I had both suspected and feared it would, the conversation turned toward Becca.

"So, how are things going with you and Becca?" Beth asked.

I shifted a bit in my seat. I liked Beth a lot, but she was still my boss, and I didn't want to say anything that would get Becca into trouble. Not that there was all that much to say, other than the fantasies I had in my head each night, which I would never talk about with anyone.

"Well, she's a great trainer. I learned a lot from her. Not only about what to do for work, or how to lead tours, but also about astronomy and other stuff," I replied, minding my words.

"Yeah, but how about after work?"

I shifted in my seat again, starting to feel uncomfortable.

"We hang out. She showed me around the night sky after we closed on my first night here. And we've hung out a bit, but nothing too serious or often," I said with caution.

"Well, judging by all the talking about you that she does, I would have guessed you were doing more than just hanging out."

She glanced over at me with a smile.

"No, we haven't..."

"Like I said the first day, as long as you keep it professional at work," she said, cutting me off. "I really don't care what you do on your own... Officially, that is."

"And unofficially?" I asked, immediately dreading the answer.

"Well," she laughed. "I think you would be a cute couple. I said that on day one, and I still believe it. She likes you, Jeremy. Trust me—I know."

"Hmm."

"And don't even pretend that you don't like her in that way. I saw the way you looked at her when you saw her for the first time that morning. I may be fun, but I'm not dumb."

She laughed a loud and braying laugh, and after a while, I joined in, relaxing and laughing with her.

We got to the reservation and pulled in front of what looked like a sports field. It had rusty bleachers arranged in a circle. A fire pit had been dug in the middle of the circle, and a stack of wood in a pyramid shape covered the pit. They had set barbecues and coolers up between the bleachers and a squat brick building. The building was identified as 'Park Office, Washrooms in back' by a sign over the front door. A set of swings was off to the north side of the circle. Looking around, I couldn't tell where the park began—it all seemed to be in the middle of the desert. There was next to no grass, but long stalks of straw and scrub surrounded it for miles.

"Unpack next to the swings," Beth instructed, gesturing toward them. "But not too close—I don't want kids kicking the telescope." She shifted her hand. "About there," she pointed.

I did as she asked and soon had the telescope set up. It was still too bright to align it with anything, but the sun was well on its way down. Aunt Gillian had been right—the sun set so late these days, it wasn't proper night until almost ten.

Beth had gone and spoken to some people who looked like they were in charge. She hugged some of them and pointed over at me. They all laughed, and Beth turned and started walking toward me.

"So, Jeremy, trial by fire," she said when she got to me. She nodded approvingly at my setup. I had set up the telescope and ladder to the east of the swings. We needed the ladder because you have to look into a telescope eyepiece exactly straight on. Think of the telescope as a big plastic tube with a mirror on one end and an eyepiece on the other. The eyepiece could be several feet in the air, depending on what you want to look at. Shorter people and kids would have trouble reaching the eyepiece without a ladder. People straining to look also tended to touch the telescope, pushing it out of alignment. People are more interested in hearing about the universe if they can see through the eyepiece. I had set up the table with Lowell-branded table cloth and our pamphlets a few yards away from the table.

"How so?" I asked. I had, after all, done public viewings plenty of times in the weeks I had been at the Observatory. I thought I knew what I was doing.

"I wasn't talking about you," she said. "This is a big annual gathering between the Hopi, my people, and the Navajo. We haven't historically been the best of friends, and recent politicking has strained relations again. We gather here, though, on the night of the solstice to tell stories about the stars and the return of the darkness. I always bring out a telescope and man it myself, but this year, they've invited me to the joint chief's council, so you'll have to stand in for me. We're trying hard to rebuild bridges between the bands."

"Okay," I replied, taking it in. "Anything in particular I should look at through the scope?"

"Start with Vega," she replied.

"Vega?" I asked. "Just a simple star?"

"The Hopi tell tales of the Blue Star that will come at the end of the world. Vega is a bright blue star, and people will want to see it. I don't think anyone really believes it. Since that will be a story told around the campfire tonight, though, it will be nice to show it to people. In fact, they will expect and ask to see it, even if just to keep an eye on it," she laughed. "After everyone finishes with Vega, you can show them interesting stuff. Ring Nebula, Andromeda, whatever you can explain interestingly. I know Becca has been teaching you stuff—time to put that to use, kid."

She grinned at me and turned to walk away.

"Oh, and don't worry, everything will be in English. The Hopi and Navajo speak distinct languages, though I expect you already knew that. Don't forget to get some food and be sure you're at the campfire at midnight so you can hear the stories, too. Educational and all," she called over her shoulder.

A warm wind blew as the sun set, and Vega, being one of the brightest stars, was one of the first we could see. Soon, I had a long line of kids and even some teens and adults who wanted to see the blue star from their legends.

As things became darker to see, I shifted from Vega to the nearby Ring Nebula. Through the telescope, it looked like a faint green smoke ring, its circular shape helping it to stand out from the background darkness. I let everyone know they were looking at what happened when a star such as ours explodes. I borrowed liberally from Dr. Tyson's 'Most Astounding Fact' YouTube video, using its poetic description of why something like this should matter to people.

Around midnight, the drums began to beat around the now-lit fire. The last glow of the sun had slipped away, and the sky was a sea of stars. Everyone turned and ran to the fire when the drums began. I saw Beth in the distance, and she waved for me to come over. I covered the aperture of the telescope so nothing would crawl into the giant tube and followed the crowd toward the fire.

We crowded the circle around the fire; people danced in the middle. Some were in traditional costume and others in street clothes. I saw a man walking toward me, and, with a grin, he pulled me into the circle of people dancing. Within seconds, I became the clumsiest and most uncoordinated person I had ever met. I tried to learn the dance as we revolved around the circle. I passed Beth, who grinned and instantly knew that she had set me up and arranged this. So, I decided not to care anymore. I let go and began to enjoy myself. Once I did, my dancing improved, and I enjoyed myself more. By the time the dancing ended, I was drenched in sweat. Several of the dancers came up and clapped me on the back or shook my hand.

"You suck, but you look like you had more fun than the rest of us combined. Thanks for participating," one lady said. They ushered me from the circle before the traditional dances began. I walked over to Beth, who shifted on the bleacher and opened up a seat for me.

A few dances later, in distinct styles with different drummers, Beth leaned over.

"They will start telling the stories now," she whispered.

The Hopi and the Navajo traded stories of creation and history for a few hours. They were all fascinating to me, not only in a historical or anthropological way, either. The storytelling of these men and women was vivid, and they sucked me into them. Finally, after midnight, an old man stood around the now smoldering fire and spoke. He sat next to Beth, so I figured he was one of the Hopi.

Mars Hill

"This is a story about the end of the world," he said in a rich baritone voice. The crowd leaned forward with anticipation. "It is the story of the Blue Star Kachina. To understand the end, we must return to the beginning. You have already heard creation stories but indulge an old man for going back to the start of things. In the beginning of time Taiwa, the Creator made his nephew so that he could build places for life to live. The nephew's name was Sotuknang. He made nine worlds—one for the Creator, one for himself, and seven worlds for the rest of life. And when life was created, it thrived. But, as has always been, we grew corrupt and wicked. The first world, Tokpela, was destroyed to wipe away the corruption, but it festered on the next two worlds, Tokpa and Kuskurza, and they followed into destruction. Each time a world was destroyed, the faithful Hopi were saved underground."

The man walked around the circle, leaning on his cane. He addressed parts of the story to people in the audience.

"Yes, those who are faithful, who are good and honest, who are not wicked or corrupt, survived. They survived to populate the next world. Today, we sit here on the fourth world—the next to be destroyed by the wickedness of men. Tuwaqachi we call this world, and its time for destruction is near. How will we know when this time will come?" he asked the crowd. "How will we know the last sign of destruction? We will hear of a dwelling in the heavens that will collapse and appear to us as a blue star. Soon after that time, the ceremonies of our people will end. The end of our people will come when the Blue Kachina removes her mask during a dance before the uninitiated children. We do not know how the world will end. It could be war, famine, disaster. Shortly after that day of purification, the True White

Brother will come to earth from the heavens. He will come to search for the Hopi who still adhere to the ancient stories and lessons; he will search the entire world for them. But, if he finds none, he will return to the stars and the earth, and everything on it will vanish forever. But, so long as there are Hopi still alive who still remember and believe in the teachings and stories, who follow our genuine way of life—well, then the world will be created anew, and all the faithful saved from the destruction."

When the story was over, everyone wanted to see Vega again, but this time with more reverence. The mood had grown solemn, and after hearing the story, I felt solemn, too. I wondered how close to the end of the world we were these days.

Soon, people drifted away toward their homes and sleep. Beth and I packed up the telescope and headed back to Flagstaff. On the way home, I thought about what was valuable in my life, and what the goal of it was. I didn't come up with any answers.

Finally, after another five weeks, on my day off, Aunt Gillian snagged me in the kitchen while I made lunch. I had just fed the cat, and she was lying on the windowsill, tail twitching through the sunbeams that shone into the kitchen. The sun reflected from the granite counters and ultramodern appliances.

"Jeremy, I have some good news!"

"Oh yeah? What's up, Aunt G?"

"You're cooking dinner tonight!"

I sighed. I cooked dinner a couple of times a week because I did enjoy cooking, and people enjoyed what I prepared for them—but I had planned on going to see a movie that afternoon, possibly having a few minutes to text Becca. My plans definitely didn't include working in the kitchen.

"Cook for four. It's going to be a celebration, so here's $200." She slipped me some cash with a wink. "Get the best steaks you can find—and pick out some good wine from the cupboard, our guest will be here at seven."

That was more interesting than cooking a random dinner at home. I was glad my aunts thought a drinking age of twenty-one was akin to tyranny. For most of the rest of the world, it was sixteen to nineteen, so they let me drink at home with them. I never got drunk, though—I'd had enough of feeling crappy for a lifetime.

That evening, I had finished the salad, and the meat was cooking nicely when I heard our guest pull into the driveway. Aunt Gillian and Aunt Sam popped into the kitchen.

"We're going to entertain our guest in the living room. Let us know when dinner's ready. Also, she doesn't know it's a surprise, so don't tell her it's a celebration dinner," Aunt Gillian said.

"Okay...Who's our guest?" I asked.

"Never you mind, Jeremy," Aunt Sam said with a grin. "It's a surprise for you, too."

My heart leaped—it had to be Becca. I rushed to finish the meal and went into the living room. Aunt Sam smiled when I walked in. Sure enough, there she was.

Becca looked happy. She gave me a huge smile, her eyes lighting up at seeing me.

"Dinner's ready," I said, my heart racing.

"Did you cook it, Jeremy?" Becca asked.

"Yes, he did," Aunt Gillian said before I could reply. "Jeremy cooks really well, and tonight he wanted to make a nice meal. I figured I'd invite my favorite student to eat my favorite nephew's cooking."

"I'm your *only* nephew," I said with a smile, a slight tremor in my voice at being so close to Becca again.

"And I'm your only student," Becca said, jumping on the bandwagon.

"Let's eat," Aunt Sam said, pulling my Aunt Gillian towards the living room.

Shyly, Becca took my hand. When our bodies touched, it felt as though static held us. She leaned her head on my shoulder. When we got to the dining room, both my aunts looked at us, grinning from ear-to-ear.

"Wow, Jeremy!" Becca said when she saw all the food on the table. "This looks fantastic."

As we ate and made small talk, Becca kept rubbing her foot up and down my leg. It turned me on. I still wasn't sure where I stood with her. I was pretty sure I wasn't just a friend by now, but where things stood from there, I still didn't know. A feeling of inexperience ran through me; I felt like a kid at a table full of adults. Before coming here, I had never even been on a date, let alone had a girlfriend and had sex.... Fucking cancer. Not only does it try to steal your future, but it also steals your present, too.

On second thought, if I had never had the cancer, I wouldn't be here now. My life verses cancer: plus one for Becca and Flagstaff, negative several billion for trying to kill me.

As we finished dessert, my Aunt G said, "I have an announcement, everyone."

We all turned to look at her. Luthien jumped into my lap, smelling for any scrap of food she might purloin. I rubbed her head and ears, grabbing an unwanted piece of fat and giving it to her.

"As you all know, Becca has been working hard on her paper about finding exoplanets. She took extra time off to finish the edits to her paper. I found out today that the IAU has accepted the paper without edits. And it's all in your name —no co-author! You did it, Becca! You're going to be published! You will present your paper at the conference in Colorado Springs in three weeks."

Becca's foot stopped mid=stroke, her fork falling from her hand. My aunts beamed with pride and pleasure. Luthien jumped from my lap to Becca's and began rubbing her head into Becca's arms. I could swear the cat was psychic.

"Congratulations," I said, turning to her with a smile. She looked utterly absent and shocked. I reached out with a bit of concern at her continued silence. I placed a hand on her shoulder.

She turned to look at me. Our knees touched now. Her brown eyes were so wide and bright; a tear fell from one.

"Are you okay?" I glanced over at my aunts, who were still smiling and acting unconcerned at Becca's silence.

"I'm...I'm published?" Becca asked me, looking right into my eyes. "On my own?"

"That's what Aunt G says," I nodded.

"But grad students don't get published. Not on their own, anyway; not even post docs get published on their own," she objected, stammering.

"Well, you should take that as a sign of how good your work is and be happy," Aunt Gillian said. Sam nodded in agreement. I gave her my most encouraging smile.

All at once, her shock broke, and a rush of feelings played out across her. Then she leaned over and kissed me—I don't think anyone expected that.

As our lips touched for the first time, sparks raced up and down my spine. The world around me faded. The first kiss was just a peck. My hand went on its own up to her cheek. We pulled apart a bit, and our foreheads rested together while we breathed. Then we kissed again—longer, deeper, more passionate.

"It's about time," Aunt Sam whispered to Aunt Gillian, who I could see nod in agreement from the corner of my eye. Maybe the kiss wasn't that unexpected, then.

I got up from the table after we had finished eating, cleared away the dinner things, and put the kettle on for some tea. Aunt Sam grabbed a plate of cookies that I had baked earlier. We all moved to the living room to relax. My aunts spoke for a few minutes about Becca's upcoming trip. Aunt G told her what she would need to do to prepare, then my aunts left us alone, under the pretense of "those who cook, do not clean." It also left Becca and me on our own for the first time in weeks.

I wondered if the kiss we had shared was just a fluke—a momentary bout of excitement. I tried not to get hard thinking about it and reliving it over and over. Becca slid closer to me on the couch, our legs touching, and rested her head on my shoulder. Yep, I was definitely hard now—I just hoped she didn't notice.

"I really missed you, Jeremy," she whispered.

"I missed you, too," I replied, the words getting caught in my suddenly dry throat.

She took my hand in hers.

"It was so lonely. Weeks at a telescope monitor at night, then getting five hours of sleep before waking up to write my thesis and then doing it all over again. I had finally finished collecting my data and started working on my thesis when Dr. Gillian told me she wanted me to do some edits on one of my papers. It must have been to reply to issues the Peer Review found, but she never told me she had submitted it for publication! God, I still can't believe it. So I did lots of re-writes and fine-tuning and handed it in to Dr. G, and now... well, here I am."

"Sounds like it's been a busy couple of months," I said. "I wish I could have seen you, but wow—you did so well."

Since I was also studying in an academic discipline where publish or perish was also very much a factor, I understood her joy. It was very rare for a student to be published without their professor's name on the paper as well.

"So, are you coming back to work?" I asked nervously. I was happy for her but worried this might mean she wouldn't come back.

"Yeah, I'm starting again next week." I grinned at her in relief, and she grabbed my head, trying to kiss me but ending up head butting me instead. We broke out laughing and tried again, only coming up for breath when my aunts came back into the room.

4

THE PHONE RANG AND RANG. It was kind of surprising for Mom not to answer on the second or third ring—she was usually the kind of person glued to her cellphone. One time, she thought she had left her cellphone at the hospital after taking me in for chemo. She had turned the car around to go back and look while I searched her purse for it. I had just started to get carsick when I spotted the phone on the floor under her legs; she must have dropped it when getting in the car.

"Hello?" I snapped out of my memories by the sound of my dad answering the phone. He never answered my mom's phone, so for half a second, I didn't recognize his voice.

"Dad?"

"Oh, hey, Jeremy. How's it hanging?"

"I'm good. Why are you answering Mom's phone?" I asked.

"Oh, she's just in the bath and didn't want to get out, so she made me answer it for her."

"Oh. I'm surprised she didn't have it with her."

"Would you believe she was charging it?"

"Isn't it like only one in the afternoon?"

"Yep. Your mom is on that phone so much these days, texting friends. She says she can't see it that well, she turns the screen up to full brightness. I swear that woman spends all day texting," Dad laughed. "You'd think she didn't know texting existed until a few weeks ago."

"I see." Amused that she had used the phone so much it had lost its battery, I was relieved that Mom seemed to have somewhat returned to normal. When I was sick, she rarely did anything on her phone that didn't involve my cancer. It was nice to hear that she was reconnecting with friends.

"So, what's up, buttercup? How have you been feeling?" Dad asked.

"I've been feeling great, actually. Sometimes I'm sore, but I think that's from working out. I sleep a lot, but less than the fourteen hours I did before. On the whole, it's so much better now."

"I figured the clean air would help—that, and getting a bit of freedom. Speaking of which, tell me about this girl," Dad said.

"Well, Aunt G and Aunt Sam and I had Becca over for dinner last night. Becca's getting published, so we had a bit of a celebration," I said.

"Does my little guy finally have a *girlfriend*?" Dad teased.

"Well... I don't know," I muttered.

"Okay, let me give you some fatherly advice. First of all, have you been on a date?"

I thought back to our trip to the lookout.

"Well, we went out to the lookout on my first night, and we have hung out a lot at work. I'm going out with her tomorrow for dinner at a new shawarma place."

I was happy I had made that date with Becca.

"Okay, so I'll check that box," Dad said. "Have you kissed her?"

"Well, it's more like she kissed me," I said, embarrassed.

"That counts double! Look, kid, I think you're on track with this girl. She seems to be content to make all the moves, which, no offense, seems to be your type."

"Yeah." He was right—I was far too timid to make the first move. I didn't want to screw it up—or worse, make her uncomfortable. The result was my paralysis.

"But I'm glad you asked her out. It shows you'll be a partner, not someone she has to manage all the time. Trust me, she will tire of making all the moves eventually. If you keep on putting your best foot forward when you can, it will show her you're not just in this for the ride."

"Thanks, Dad. I don't know what this is, I just... really like her. I think I'm falling for her."

"It's like you Zinged," he said.

"The girls are making you watch Hotel Transylvania again?"

"I swear they have it on repeat—I'm starting to recite it every time I close my eyes."

I actually liked the H.T. movies a lot. There was something about the kind of love Mavis and Jonathan had in that movie that made me feel kind of jealous. I wanted something like that.

"Well, I hope something else catches their interest soon," I said, showing him some support.

"It's difficult being the only man in the house," Dad joked, but I saw through it.

"I miss you too, Dad."

"Did you still want to talk to your mother?"

"No, I got some expert advice from you—tell her and the girls I say 'what's up.'" The phrase drove my mother insane. She always nagged me to be more formal with my language when talking to her and the girls.

Dad laughed. "I'll translate that to 'Jeremy says Hello' for you."

"Thanks, Dad."

"Love you, Jeremy."

"Love you too. Bye," I said, disconnecting the call.

As I was putting my phone back in my pocket, I got a text from Becca.

Becca: Doing anything tomorrow before our shawarma date?

Me: Was going to study, but otherwise not much. Why?

Becca: Do you think you can be up super early tomorrow? Like 5 AM?

Me: Sure. Why?

Becca: Surprise for you. I'll pick you up at 5. Wear warm clothes. Oh, and bring some cool clothes too, and a few sandwiches and a couple bottles of water.

Me: Another surprise outing, hmm? And a strange packing list. You intrigue me. I'm in. See you then!

It was colder than I expected the next morning, so I was glad Becca had suggested the warm clothes. I sat on the front step of my aunt's house and sipped warm tea from a thermos as I waited for Becca to arrive. I looked up at the stars as they slipped behind the warm yellow glow of the rising sun. I recognized the constellation Cygnus overhead as the wind rustled through the trees. After a few minutes, Becca pulled up, and I jumped into the passenger seat.

"Good morning, Becca."

"Good morning to you, too."

"You going to tell me what this surprise is yet?"

"Nope," she said, her smile reflecting the soft lighting of the dashboard. I sighed and took another sip from my thermos.

"Coffee?" Becca asked hopefully.

"No, jasmine tea."

"Ugh. I forgot you don't drink coffee. Can I have some anyway? I left my thermos at home."

"Sure thing," I said, handing her the thermos. "It's hot, so be careful."

"Thanks," she said, after taking a long pull of the tea.

"No problem."

We drove through the silent early morning streets of Flagstaff before turning toward the north and leaving the city behind us.

"It should be a nice day," Becca said. "I'm back at work tomorrow, and now I get to spend my last day off with you as my reward for going back to work."

"Thanks. It's always a pleasure to spend time with you too, m'lady," I said with a laugh. Her words flattered me.

"I rarely drive with no music, by the way," she said, sounding a little self-conscious. "It's just that…"

"Just what?" I asked when she stopped talking.

"Just that I want today to be perfect, and I don't want to ruin it by playing a stupid song or something."

I laughed. "I'm sure I'll love whatever you put on. I've got a wide taste in music. In fact, I'll make it a game—try to find a song I don't like."

She smiled. "Okay then, challenge accepted." She hit a button on her car stereo.

The sounds of Dr. Jones by Aqua flooded the car.

"A good wake-me-up song," I said with a laugh and sang along.

"Really?"

"Hey, I memorize music easily," I blurted before starting up again.

She laughed and then started singing too. We were still blasting music from the late '90s as we pulled into an empty parking lot. A wide-open clearing in the trees appeared in front of us. The glow of the sun highlighting the mountains peaks surrounding us cast long shadows through the trees.

Silence descended as we parked the car.

"I can't believe you knew the words to all those songs," Becca said, opening her door and stepping out of the car onto the crunchy gravel of the parking lot.

"I don't know how I do it. I guess I learn music fast," I said, as I stepped out too, closing the car door behind me. I put my thermos in the side pocket of my backpack before slinging it over my shoulder.

"But those songs were retro when *I* heard them. They're like, super retro for you!"

"Would it surprise you to learn that I first heard all those '90s pop songs from Aunt G?"

Becca stared at me from across the roof of her car.

"Actually, no," she said. "I can believe that 100 percent," she grinned, reaching in and pulling out her own backpack and two hiking poles. Coming around the front of the car, she tossed one of the poles to me.

"Surprise," Becca said with a grin. "We're going to try to hike to the summit of Mount Humphrey—the highest point in Arizona."

I laughed. "Are you trying to get out of our shawarma date by making me die of fatigue first?" I teased.

She grinned. "I'm only making sure you're hungry for it." Her face turned serious. "But we don't have to if you don't want."

"Becca, relax. Let's give it a go. I can't promise I can make it the whole way, but I'm game to try."

She looked relieved and excited. "Good. Let's get started, then," she said. She stepped off along a trail at the edge of the parking lot, heading across the clearing. I only now saw that chairlifts ran through the empty area, leading up the slope.

"Is this a ski hill?" I asked.

"Yep. I've only been once or twice with classmates."

"I've only skied a few times, too, but on bunny hills compared to this. If I'm around this winter, we should come."

"Consider it a date," Becca said, turning and grabbing my hand. We walked across the clearing and into the trees, holding hands. It wasn't long until we hit our first switchback. We didn't say much as we climbed the trail heading up the mountain. Birds called around us, and a breeze rustled the trees. I loved the smell of the grass, ski hill, and fresh air. I had thought the air in Flagstaff had been pretty clean and fresh, especially compared to Chicago, but now that I was out in nature, it was fresher still. After an hour or so, we stopped seeing parts of the ski runs on every other switchback. Twenty minutes later, we came to what looked like a still river of rocks running down the slope.

"Let's take a breather," Becca said, panting.

"If you like," I replied, trying to keep my own panting down. I was glad she had called the stop because I was about to ask for one myself.

We sat on some rocks and looked out at the valley below, which had emerged from shadows as the sun had risen. We both pulled off our sweatshirts and stuffed them in our backpacks. The temperature had risen with the sun; I had a feeling the day might be a scorcher.

"Look at the mountains out there. I never thought about Arizona having volcanos, but it's cool to see them," I said. I pointed at the cinder cone peaks in the distance. "It's quite the view." I turned to look at Becca as I opened my water bottle and took a drink.

"I'll drink to that," she said, and we toasted with our water bottles.

I reached out and took her hand again, and we sat for a short while.

"Want to keep going?"

"Sure," I said, standing and putting my backpack on. I gasped as the weight of it pressed my sweat-covered shirt onto my back.

Becca grinned at me and swung her backpack onto her shoulders, too, wincing as it did the same to her. I smiled at her, and she reached up and pulled me down for a kiss. Her lips were chapped, and I suspected mine were, too. It didn't matter though—I was kissing Becca again. My heart leaped in my chest, and as the kiss ended, I was sure I had a dazed smile on my face.

Becca turned and started up the trail, and I followed. Soon, it got warm, and I wished I could change into my shorts. We climbed and climbed, the trees becoming shorter and smaller. Finally, we broke from the tree line with nothing ahead of us but rocky slopes. Once clear of the trees, it felt like the temperature dropped twenty degrees. Now I had an unobstructed view of the summit—our goal. It seemed so close.

"Let's take a breather," I said, dropping to the ground and rubbing my sore legs. We'd been climbing for hours now; I was past feeling the burn, my muscles instead starting to feel like jello. I was also sweating hard, despite the continued coolness of the shade and altitude.

"Sure," Becca said, sitting next to me and rubbing her own legs. She leaned over and rested her head on my shoulder. It surprised me how well we seemed to fit together. I reached my arm and put it around her waist. I saw her smile from the corner of my eye. I had been nervous that somehow, everything up to this point was a coincidence, and that maybe she just wanted to be friends. My rational brain knew I was being stupid—I mean, she had kissed me several times now for crying out loud. Still, deep down, I worried she might not be receptive to me touching her.

I don't know how long we sat like that. It felt like hours, but it also felt like no time at all.

"All right, lazy bones—let's go," Becca said, standing. "Daylight's a-wasting."

"You good to try to make it to the top?" I said, leaning on my borrowed hiking pole.

"Sure, we came all this way, didn't we? It would be a shame to give up so close to the finish line."

Well, we weren't as close as we thought. I followed Becca along the narrow path. It ran up a ridge and then along the steep surface of the mountain and toward the summit. I tried not to look to my left toward the sharp drop, or to my right at the climb still ahead of us.

Come on, Jeremy, one step in front of the other, I said to myself.

A dull ache throbbed in the center of my brain. I pushed it away, pulling the water from my backpack and taking a swig. I kept moving, but to my horror, Becca pulled ahead of me. The gap between us opened over the next half hour. I tried to keep pushing on, trying to close the gap, but it seemed like the harder I tried, the more I sweat and the stronger the headache became. I couldn't even see Becca ahead of me anymore as the path forward curved out of sight.

I saw a wider part of the path about twenty feet ahead. All I had to do was make it those twenty feet, and I would rest for a bit and try to get my breathing under control. It felt like it took an hour to make it those twenty feet. I dropped to the ground, panting, not even bothering to take off my backpack. My head was killing me. I closed my eyes and focused on my breath to keep it under control. I must have dozed off because the next thing I remember, someone shook me awake.

"Jeremy?" A sweet voice said, as though coming through a long tunnel. "Jeremy, are you okay? Come on, talk to me."

The shaking became stronger, and I felt myself snap back awake.

"Woah," I said. "Becca?"

"Jeremy, you scared me. Are you okay? I couldn't get you to wake up."

"To be honest, I'm actually feeling pretty crappy."

"Let's turn around, then. You might have altitude sickness."

Becca tugged at my arm, and I gritted my teeth together as I pulled myself up.

Becca helped me as best she could to walk down the narrow path.

It was startling how fast I felt better the more we descended. My headache was completely gone by the time we reached the tree line. Going down felt like it took no time at all.

"Let's take another break," Becca said, setting her backpack down under the shade of a tree.

"Sure," I said, sitting beside her. We both leaned against the hard bark of the tree. "I'm sorry."

"It's okay," she said, turning to look at me. "I'd rather come back and try another day than risk you getting sick or hurt."

"Can I come?"

"What?"

"Can I come with you when you try it again? The mountain may have beaten me today, but I want to give it another go."

Becca laughed. "I'm just relieved that you're okay. I don't think I could have carried you down the mountain."

I smiled back at her. "I'm sure you would have managed. You're pretty strong, you know."

She elbowed me in the ribs softly. "And don't you forget it," she laughed.

The scorching summer sun shone down on Becca and me later that evening as we walked along the main street through town. I hadn't known this when I moved here, but you can't walk the streets of Flagstaff without knowing that the Main Street is Historic Route 66; every store and city sign seemed to brag about it.

"So, I have to admit," Becca said, reaching out and taking my hand, "that I've never had shawarma before."

"You're kidding!"

"No, seriously. I've had doner before, but never shawarma."

"You'll love it," I said. I pushed open the door to the restaurant, feeling the air conditioning blasting out into the street.

As soon as I walked into the store, I could smell the spice, onions, and parsley. Vertical skewers of meat slowly turned in front of a heater ahead of us, their outsides crispy. I knew that inside the meat would be moist and dissolve in your mouth.

"What do you suggest?" Becca asked me, looking up at the menu over the counter.

"I usually go for the chicken and lamb platter, with rice, salad, and Tahini sauce," I said, looking for the platter number on the menu.

"Sounds good to me," Becca said, stepping up to the counter and ordering.

We stood in silence as the food was prepared. We each paid and took our trays from the man behind the counter. We moved through the crowded dining area and over to an empty booth against the far wall of the store.

"How are you feeling?" Becca asked as we sat.

"Much better than this morning. Like you said, going down helped. I also took a nap, and I feel back to normal now."

"Normal? My legs are killing me," she said with a sigh.

"Well, aside from that, I guess," I smiled and looked at her plate of untouched food. "Try it."

She scooped some meat onto her fork and popped it into her mouth.

"Well?" I asked nervously. It would be a shame if she hated one of my favorite foods.

"Oh my god. This is amazing!" she said, eating another forkful. "Why haven't I ever had this before?" she asked with a full mouth.

I laughed and tried some myself. It was every bit as fantastic as I had hoped. It was amazing to have shawarma this good in such a small town.

"Glad you like it. Shawarma is one of my favorite foods. I haven't had it much in the last few years, so I'm glad you like it 'cause I plan to eat it a lot."

"Why didn't you have it much recently?"

"Well... When I was sick, I threw up a lot. I never wanted to throw up shawarma because I love it so much, so I figured it was better not to eat it at all than it would be to ruin it. To this day, I still hate bananas—allegedly, they taste the same if you throw them up; they don't."

My cheeks flushed. "Sorry," I added, "didn't mean to gross you out while you're eating."

"It's okay."

We ate in silence. After a while, I felt uncomfortable again. Did I ruin our date? Oh, man... I really screwed this one up. I continued to sink into a whirlpool of self-recrimination and anxiety as I methodically worked on emptying my plate.

"You know, I've been thinking..." Becca said. I looked up at her and noticed her plate was already empty, "...we're kind of different."

My heart sank further.

"But, in like, the right way, if you know what I mean," she said, as if she could read my heart sinking on my face.

"What do you mean?"

"Well," she began, "there are the obvious things. I'm a scientist, you're a historian. I'm studying for my doctorate, and you're an undergrad. I'm Australian, and you're American. I grew up on a farm, you grew up in the city."

"Yeah, that's true," I replied, wondering where she was going with this.

"We grew up in such different worlds. By rights, we should never have met—we're so different. I'm kind of in awe that in a small town at a fork in the road, I met you. You know that old saying, that opposites attract? I kind of don't believe it because we're not actually opposites. It's kind of a miracle we're sitting here today."

"I don't know what to say," I said, breathless.

Becca laughed her wind chime laugh.

"You don't have to say anything; it's just that I never thought I'd..." she cut herself off, flushing.

"You never thought...?" I prompted.

"Never mind. This food was superb; thank you so much for sharing it with me. I better get home soon and get ready for work tomorrow."

"Oh. Okay, yeah, of course. Sorry," I said, picking up our trays and dropping them off at the tray return station.

"Don't be sorry. Thank you for bringing me here, Jeremy. And for going on that hike with me this morning. You sure you're feeling okay?"

"Yeah, I feel fine," I said, as we stepped back out into the heat. "I'm glad you invited me for the hike. You sure you don't want to get some ice cream or something for dessert?"

"No, that's okay, I'm actually getting kind of tired. I should head home."

"Okay, Becca. I'll see you tomorrow."

She reached up and hugged me, pulling me down for a kiss,

"Sorry, Jeremy. I had a wonderful time and can't wait till we do this again—really."

"I know. Big day tomorrow."

"G'night, Jeremy."

"G'night, Becca."

She turned and walked away.

I sighed, confused. I thought it had been going well. I don't know what happened.

The Lowell staff threw a little party for Becca in the break room on her first day back.

I staggered around cleaning up afterward, barely able to walk after the hike the day before. Once everyone had said their congratulations and gone to get ready for the first visitors of the day, Becca came up to me.

"I'm sorry," she said.

"For what?"

"For how last night ended. It wasn't fair. I feel like I ruined our date. Can we pretend that never happened?"

"It's okay. I know it's been a stressful few months for you. And pretend that what never happened?" I asked with a wink.

Becca smiled and hugged me. "Thanks, Jeremy."

She pulled me down for a quick kiss. As we pulled apart, the break room door opened, and Beth walked in.

"I'm sure nothing was happening in here other than you two cleaning up. Hurry up, we've got people pulling into the parking lot— I need my tour guides looking presentable and ready to go," she said with a stern voice but a goofy grin. "Let's go, lovebirds."

We fell right back into the groove we were in before Becca left for her telescope time. Over the next few weeks, we split the tour duties again. Whenever we cleaned something away from prying eyes, we took the opportunity. Every observing night, the two of us would try to work the Clark telescope together. Failing that, we would set up portable telescopes next to each other, working back-to-back, showing people around the universe.

We kept talking after that. Hopes and dreams. Jokes. Likes and dislikes. We couldn't get enough of each other. I kept trying to get up the nerve to ask her if we were in an 'official' relationship—after all, we'd hugged, kissed, and held hands. I still didn't know if we were an 'us,' but I never could get the words out.

One Tuesday in July, Becca asked me to meet her down at the university. We met in the local café, and she took me to the walk-in clinic.

"What are we doing here?" I asked her.

"We're going to do this right, so we're going to get tested."

"Tested? For what?"

She gave me a sideways glance and then grinned at me, flicking her eyes to a sign that read "Free community STD testing TODAY" on the clinic door.

Then I understood. The sun was blistering, and I was already feeling sweaty in my T-shirt and jeans—my fear of needles had nothing to do with it. They called us in one at a time. The university was doing a free STD screening clinic for anyone in the community, as long as the health studies students did the practical work. The tech I had got the needle in on the first try, which was pain-free and an enormous relief to me; I'd had enough needles for a lifetime.

When Becca walked out, she had a Band-Aid on each arm. "Took them like five times to get it in a vein," she sniffed.

"Ouch!"

"Ouch? It was me getting stuck with those damn needles, Jer."

"Want me to kiss and make it better?"

"Yeah, okay," she said with a goofy grin.

She was full of surprises, but a promise was a promise, so I kissed her arms. I then held her by the waist and gave her a long kiss on the lips, our tongues dancing together. When we pulled apart, we both gasped for air and laughed. I had gotten used to flirting, kissing, and touching her over the last few weeks. If I weren't careful, I would be one of those PDA freaks that my mom always looked down her nose at.

"Doing anything Friday night?" she asked me.

"Nope."

"Good. I'll be by your place at eight—pack warm clothes."

Work that week went by in a blur. On Thursday, we got our STD screening results back. We were both clean, and while I had no doubts about me, it was always nerve-wracking to find out the results, anyway; I'd had too many terrible test results to be comfortable until I knew—there was always a chance something had slipped through the screening for one of my blood transfusions. It was likewise good to know that Becca was clean, too, even though all we did was kiss.

Friday at eight, I sat in shorts and a T-shirt on our front porch. Both Aunt Sam and Aunt Gillian were working, so there was nothing left for me to do but hang out and enjoy the sunset. Becca arrived soon after, and I jumped in the car, tossing my backpack and jacket in the back.

"All ready to go?" she asked.

"Yep, where are we going?"

"It's a surprise."

"You must enjoy taking me out on surprises."

We went north from town, holding hands while we drove into the desert. We listened to music and chatted on the hour ride. An old dirt road turned off the highway, and we went on for another ten minutes before we came to a gate. Becca got out and unlocked it, then we drove inside.

She locked the gate behind us, and we finally arrived at a large, flat area of grass in the desert. By now, the sun was a glow on the horizon, and millions of stars stretched out over our heads in the warm summer evening.

I stared around us when we got out of the car, and then looked up into the depths of space. "Where are we?"

"This is some land Beth's family owns. I told her I needed a break and wanted to get out of town for a bit, and she said I could come here and camp for the night. She even loaned me camping supplies. Before it gets dark, we should set up the tent and fire pit. Beth said there was one already dug here somewhere. How about you go try find it, and I'll start unpacking? We'll set up the tent near the fire, but I want to leave the car here by the gate—Beth asked us not to drive too far into the campsite."

I started walking towards the middle of the clearing and almost fell into the fire pit. I was a city boy, so when people say 'fire pit' in relation to a campground, I think of a little metal stand or a ring of rocks people have in their backyards. This was definitely not what I was expecting.

An Arizona 'fire pit' was apparently two or three-feet deep in the middle and about six-feet across. There were no rocks to make the edge obvious, but there was still ash and some burned wood down at the bottom, which made it clear this was what I was looking for. It was a lot more like the tribal fire pit, which was twice the size of this one than a traditional campground fire pit.

"I think I found it!" I called over to Becca, fifty feet away.

"Cool! Come help me haul the wood."

I walked back and saw that she had enough supplies to build a tiny village. She began stacking logs in my outstretched arms. "Why did you bring so much wood?"

"Beth gave it to me. She said we would need it to have a proper camping trip. She knows the land, so I didn't argue."

We carried the first load over to the fire pit, and Becca expertly built a tee-pee from the logs. "Just like being in the Outback."

"Hopefully, fewer venomous snakes and spiders, though," I laughed.

"Well, not as severe, but there are still some out here. Don't worry though, nothing here wants to hurt us, and they've probably moved away by now, anyway. We're scarier to them than they are to us. If you see anything, leave it alone and give it room—it won't hurt you."

I kept near the fire, just in case.

"One small candle casts a little light. One small candle takes away the night. So much darkness, small bright light, you know the darkness cannot stand the light," she crooned to herself. She used a long match to get the fire going. She coaxed the flames into a warm, crackling fire, which built and grew towards the sky.

The next step was to get the tent set up and sleeping bags unrolled inside. We finished just as the last glow of the sun faded away. Becca brought out two folding chairs and two beers.

"To your success," I said toasted as we clinked our bottles together.

"I don't know what I did to deserve this," she smiled at me and then looked up at the stars.

I followed her gaze. The Milky Way was right overhead, running from north to south. She took my free hand while we sat side-by-side by the warm fire, drinking our cold beers.

"What do you mean?"

"I never thought I would drop my emotional walls enough to feel this way about someone. My sister is coming to live with me, and I'm being published, which is one step closer to getting my Ph.D... It's all lining up for me."

"Becca, you busted your ass for this. You work harder than anyone I know. You are the kindest, sweetest, funniest girl I've ever loved, and I can't imagine anything but happiness for you."

"You love me?" she asked, her voice shaky. Flames reflected from the moisture rimming her rich eyes as she looked at me.

"Yeah... I guess... From the moment I first saw you. I know it's cliché. I feel like I've known you my entire life, and that we're meant to be together."

"You don't mind me being five years older than you?" she asked.

"Shit, a year ago, I didn't think I was going to even live five more years. But what is it, really? You're older than me. You're smarter than me; you're definitely prettier than me. But what does that matter? I love you. I've never felt this way about anyone before. I don't know why I waited this long to tell you."

"Me, too," Becca said. She set her beer down and stood. "I've been a fool," she knelt in front of me. "When I was a girl, I promised myself that when I finally fell in love for the first time, I would tell him right away. Why wait to tell someone you love them? Isn't it better to err on the side of love than on the side of fear? And it scared me, Jeremy. Not you," she said, looking me in the eyes, "but of letting myself go enough to even think about being with someone again. But I don't want to be afraid. I love you too, Jeremy. I felt it the moment you literally shocked me on your first day—and I will not let love frighten me. That's what I was trying to say on that shawarma date I messed up. No, don't," she said, leaning forward to kiss me when I tried to reply.

Her lips were warm and soft as they met mine. She opened her mouth, and I followed her lead as our tongues danced. When we came up for air, she sat on my lap, and we leaned back and looked up into the universe. Then I looked into her eyes and kissed her again. I rubbed her back as she turned and straddled me, slowly grinding into my growing erection. I reached under her sweater and shirt and rubbed her back as she pressed herself into me.

5

"Fuck! Your hands are icy!" she gasped. She pushed my arms down until they were clear of her shirt.

I felt my heart drop when she hopped up and pulled her sweater down, but then she reached down and grabbed my hand.

"Come on." She pulled me into the tent, our beers and the universe forgotten in our desire for each other.

I zipped the tent closed and turned to face her. The light of the fire bled through the yellow canvas, so I had no trouble seeing at all.

She immediately jumped on me and kissed me. Her hands went from around my neck to the zipper of my sweater. Within seconds, I was topless. The cold made my nipples stand on end, while the chilly air on my back contrasted with the warmth of her hands as she ran her fingers down my back. We drew apart, and in another few seconds, she had me completely naked. She stood back and looked me over with a hunger in her eyes.

I knew she could see my scars, but her eyes slid over them. She didn't run away screaming, as I had feared she might.

"I've been wanting this for so long," she muttered, taking my hands and guiding them to her breasts.

I couldn't feel very much through the multiple layers of her jacket and sweater, so I pulled her into a kiss and started taking off her clothes. She helped me with the first two layers, and then a T-shirt. I grabbed the bottom hem, pulling upwards in one motion, revealing her purple bra. I fumbled at it, trying to take it off. She grinned and reached around her back, and in a heartbeat, she had pulled it off and cast it aside.

Her breasts were wonderful. Two slight rises on her chest with dark areolas and pencil-eraser nipples, erect and pointing at me. I pulled her to me in another kiss, and the warmth of our bellies touching skin-to-skin seemed to set us both on fire. I reached out and cupped her left breast in my right hand. It was supple, warm, firm, and wonderful; I could have stared at them for hours, studying their every detail.

She leaned in and kissed me again. Then she pulled me to the floor where our sleeping bags lay zipped together—something she must have done at some point—they were open enough for us to get in together, though. She pulled my head down from our kiss to her breast, and I took her nipple in my mouth.

I used my tongue to play with her while she panted in pleasure. Before long, she moved me to her other breast. I smelled a scent I wasn't familiar with as she became more aroused. It was musty and smelled wonderful. I ran my hand up her thigh towards her abdomen while my tongue played with her nipple.

"Let me take this off," she said, and started undoing her belt. Her pixie-like body wriggled while she kicked the last few inches of her pants off her feet. Her socks went next.

I was in rapture. I couldn't believe this was finally happening. She pulled off her underwear, and at last, I saw her naked before me. Her skinny legs parted a little as she pulled me back for another kiss.

She reached out and wrapped her hand around my now erect penis. The touch of her warm and smooth hand on it was like magic. It was all I could do not to cum at her first touch.

I reached between her legs and followed the heat to her moist core. She grabbed my hand, showing me what she liked. First, she dipped a finger into her and then pulled the wet tip to her clit. She made me touch the area around it, and soon I rubbed it while she played with my dick. With my other hand, I propped myself up and leaned forward to kiss her again.

Her eyes opened, and it was like seeing the depths of the universe in them. I then kissed my way down her body until I got to her clit.

"I've never done this before," I admitted, looking up at her again.

"I'm sure you'll figure it out," she panted, and she spread her legs for me.

I reached out with my tongue. I lapped at her clit, and she moaned with delight. I had no clue what I was doing, so I started drawing the letters of the alphabet with my tongue on her hard nub. I reached up to play with her breasts at the same time.

After a few minutes, she clenched her legs, holding my head in place while she made a high squeal that turned into a low moan and panting. She finally relaxed, and I could get a breath of air. Then I lay down beside her.

"Thanks for that. It's been a very long time since I felt this good." Becca got on her knees then. I started to get up myself, but she said, "Lie down—I'll return the favor."

With that, she took me into her mouth. The warmth of it was a shock after the coldness of the air. She took me in and began bobbing her head up and down. Her tongue whipped around the head of my dick, occasionally playing with the very tip. I could feel the bumpy texture of her tongue while she worked it around me. She then popped my dick out of her mouth with a gasp and began licking up and down the shaft.

"Cum for me," she said, before taking me back in her mouth and licking the head of my penis again.

The pressure in my balls started to build. All it took was for her to lick around the head a few more times before I shot my load down her throat. She swallowed what seemed like a mountain of my cum before I was finally spent. I flopped back onto the ground and saw stars while I caught my breath.

"I've never... That was... Thank you," was all I could say, panting for breath, my mind reeling at what had happened. She lay down beside me and grabbed my hand, bringing it to her clit. Getting what she wanted, I played with it again.

She stroked my dick back to life. Within a minute or two of her working on me, I was hard again. I worried I would screw this whole night up as I remembered something I should have thought of before. I looked up at her. "Um, I don't have any condoms."

"Don't worry about that—I have an IUD, and we got tested," she smiled and lay on her back, spreading her legs. "I trust you, Jer."

This is it, I thought to myself while I crawled between them, our bodies fitting together perfectly.

She took the head of my dick and guided me to her opening. She rubbed it up and down to coat it in her juices. She was soft, warm, and more slippery than I had imagined. Then she lined me back up with her and tilted her hips. Suddenly, the head of my dick was inside. She wrapped her legs around me and pulled me into her until I was fully engulfed inside.

I exhaled, enjoying the feeling. It was hot and moist, slick and velvety—tighter than I would have imagined, and unlike anything I had ever felt before. I looked down into her eyes and kissed her. Then I looked down at her belly and realized I was inside her. I almost exploded right then and there. The most beautiful woman I had ever seen. The first woman I ever loved. The smartest, kindest, funniest, and most beautiful person I knew, and I was having sex—no—making love to her.

She rocked her hips up to me, and I moved deeper within her. I withdrew and then plunged back into her warmth again and again until we built up a rhythm.

I'm pleased to say I only popped out of her maybe three or four times, but each time, she guided me back inside. When we were really going again, I looked down at her body. Her small breasts moved with each of my thrusts. Her lips twisted into a grimace of pleasure, and I kissed her while her warm and wet vagina massaged my dick. I felt the pressure growing again in my balls when she pushed me out of her and flipped over onto her hands and knees.

I pushed back into her and found that in the new position, it was much easier to go faster. I continued to thrust, and I reached underneath her to massage her breasts. She laid her head down on her arms and pushed back at me for each thrust into her. I used my now free hand to play with her clit.

She cried out into her arms, her back and legs covered in sweat—mine, hers, or both, I couldn't tell.

Again, the pressure built. I grabbed her and flipped us over so she was astride me, turning her so we would be face-to-face. Her breasts bounced as she rode me. I could get my breath back and let the feelings wash over me. After a while, I flipped us so that she lay on her back, and I was on top.

I thrust two or three more times and then grunted, "Love... You," looking into her eyes.

Time stood still. I could feel her heartbeat in her vagina, the pulse of it rippling down her tunnel and engulfing my dick. Her fully dilated eyes looked into mine, the fire reflecting the white flecks in her chocolate eyes. They were as deep as a waterfall and as expressive as an ocean. Sweat ran down my back, the icy air freezing my toes.

Finally, I came. I could feel the cum rushing up my dick. Just as it reached the tip, time snapped back, and I buried myself all the way. Then I pumped cum into her.

We were both spent. It was all we could do to zip the sleeping bag closed before we fell asleep, wrapped in each other's arms, face-to-face, nose-to-nose, cheek-to-cheek, and fell asleep.

We dozed well into the morning, pressed together, holding hands under the sleeping bag. Eventually, her cellphone alarm went off, and we got dressed. We packed up the campsite and drove back into Flagstaff, holding hands the entire way.

While we drove listening to her 90s pop music with the windows down, I thought about the previous night, what it had felt like. What it had meant to me.

I took stock of what I knew. Here I was, in love with a smart and beautiful woman who had spent the night with me. I worried, though. What would I say to my parents when I told them I would not come home? Because I now realized there was no way I was moving anywhere without her.

Could I get into the NAU history program? Would my aunts let me stay with them? Would Becca and I move in together? What about Becca's sister? Weren't she and Becca moving in together?

My thoughts raced. My hands were sweaty. A sharp stab of pain, like something snapping in my chest, and then the familiar and unwelcome feeling of adrenaline coursed through my body. My hands shook.

"You okay?" Becca asked, glancing over at me for a moment before returning her eyes to the road.

"I... I don't know what to do next. I've never been in a relationship before. What are we supposed to do now?"

I started using my breathing techniques to calm an oncoming panic attack before it started. Deep breaths, trying to keep a smooth in and out pace.

Becca laughed. "Well, how about we get back to town, and then we can sit down and talk about it?" She gave my hand a squeeze and said in a softer voice, "I promise, there is nothing for you to worry about."

I smiled and breathed deeply a few more times. I felt the adrenaline shutting off, and I calmed down.

"Sorry," I said after another few calming breaths. "Sometimes, if I get overwhelmed, I get panic attacks. A nice leftover from the anemia and cancer."

"It's okay—I get them too, sometimes," she said, reaching out to take my hand and locking her fingers through mine.

We pulled up in front of my aunts' house as Aunt Sam walked through the door. She smiled at us, holding the door open.

Becca sat at the kitchen island on a stool while I cooked breakfast.

"Did you guys have a nice time?" Aunt Sam asked.

"Yes, we did. I'll have to be sure to send Beth a text thanking her for letting us use her campsite," Becca replied.

Aunt Sam looked over at me and raised her eyebrows.

"What?" I mouthed at her.

She winked at me. "You two are good for each other." She filled up her water bottle and then went upstairs to bed.

"So, you wanted to talk about something?" Becca nervously said when we were alone again.

"Becca, I love you. And last night was... I can't even describe how great it was," I started. "But I don't know what I'm doing."

"How so?"

"I've never... Well, I've never felt this way about anyone. In the movies, the guy usually either proposes, runs away, or gets killed right about now. I don't know what I'm supposed to do. My heart is telling me there's no way I can go home in the fall. There's no way I want to leave you to go back to school in Chicago. But your sister is coming out here, and you have school and work, and your thesis. Not to mention, I have to finish my undergrad work and then go on to grad school, too, if I'm lucky. So what's our future going to be? I don't know if my aunts will let me stay here."

A muffled laugh from the top of the stairs, followed by a giggly conversation, floated down to us.

"Shut up!"

"No, you shut up, Sam!"

"Don't worry, Jer, you can stay here as long as you want," Aunt Gillian called.

"I'm trying to have a conversation here, you guys. Some privacy, please!" I called back up at them.

Becca smiled at me with warmth in her eyes.

"So, yeah..." I continued, "...I don't know what I'm supposed to be doing here."

"Well..." she whispered, "I don't know, either. Yes, my sister is coming, but that doesn't mean you can't live with us if you want to. And yes, I have another year or two to go before I finish my thesis—but, if you came to school here, that would mean we would graduate about the same time. If you go on to grad school, well... I'll be looking for a university to teach at. Maybe we could move back to Australia, or maybe we could find a school we can be at together. But the thing is, Jeremy, I love you. I want to be with you—I don't mean we should get married or engaged right now, but yeah, eventually, maybe, if things work out. But, if you stay here, it will be up to you."

"There's no question in my mind that I want to stay with you, Becca," I said.

"So stay," she said, leaning forward to kiss me.

As our lips met, I could have sworn I heard my aunts cheering.

Becca had been back at work a few weeks when she came over to me as I put away cleaning supplies.

"Hey, Jer, I have a bit of a problem."

"Anything I can help with?" I grunted as I lifted a container of dirty water to pour into the sink.

"Well, my sister, Abby—you remember, she was planning on coming to university here and moving in with me?"

"Yeah."

"Well, turns out she's not coming. Taking a gap year, I guess. She might have met some guy or something. Problem is I've already signed the lease on our apartment and given notice that I'm leaving my current place."

"So..." I wondered if this conversation would head where I thought it would.

"So..." she said, a faint blush growing on her very cute cheeks. A lock of her brown hair swung in front of her face in a way that I couldn't have found more attractive. She looked down at her shoes, building some courage. She looked back up and locked eyes with me.

"... I was wondering if you might want to move in with me?"

My heart leaped. I wondered what my aunts would think, then decided I didn't care. I felt guilty about it for a minute, though—after all, they had taken me in and given me a place to stay rent-free, and had been nothing but nice to me. But then I realized they might like to have the house to themselves.

If I moved in with her, I would have to commit to spending the next year of school here. I would have to transfer my credits over, and I would have to tell my mom I was staying. I wondered how she would take it.

Becca looked even more embarrassed.

"I mean, if you can't, don't worry—I'm sure I can find a roommate or something. I know this is kind of rushing things…"

I reached out and interrupted her, cupping her cheek, stroking it with my thumb.

"Hey, yeah, of course I'll move in with you. I mean, I know it's fast and everything, but yes, I think living with you would be a dream come true. Plus, we wouldn't have to look over our shoulders before we have sex." I reached out and took her by the waist, pulling her close. "We could do it every day if we wanted."

"Oh, thank you. I would have been in a real bind if I didn't have someone to share with. And you're right—we can christen the house whenever we want." She stood on tiptoe and whispered, "That means we have sex in every room," answering my confused look before dropping back down.

She grinned up at me, and I stole a quick kiss before putting away the rest of my cleaning supplies and going back to work in leading the next tour.

"You're glowing," Beth said to me as we prepared to lock up. "Have been all afternoon. What's going on?"

"I'm moving in with Becca."

"Good for you! I'm sure your aunts will be ecstatic."

They were ecstatic, then reassured me they would be happy for me to keep living with them, just in case I thought they were glad to get rid of me.

Things didn't quite go as well with my mom.

"What do you mean you're moving in with a girl and not coming home? Jeremy, you're going too fast. I mean, have you even thought about this? We were expecting you at the end of the month. And what about your doctor's appointments? The people here know you and your case, Jeremy. You still need follow-up and regular tests."

It had been like this for twenty minutes with no let-up. I sighed and gripped the phone tighter, trying to keep the frustration from my voice.

"It's exactly what it sounds like, Mom. I like it here, and I want to stay for the school year. It's a beautiful city. I have a job, and I'm working on getting into the university. Aunt Sam set me up with a contact at the school. We already have my application for transfer submitted—and, as surprising as this might sound, they have doctors here too. It will be fine."

"This seems too fast. Too sudden. Does Gillian know this girl?"

"Yes, Mom, Rebecca is her student, remember? They've known each other for years."

"Well, I just don't know."

Aunt G had expected something like this and had given me a tip to help convince my parents that it was a good idea.

"Well, why don't you come out here and meet her? Aunt G already said you can stay over with her and Sam. I'll have already moved, so the guest room is free. And we can show you around."

"I don't know, Jeremy. I'm not comfortable with this."

Sigh. "Can I talk to Dad?" I asked.

It took a few more minutes before Dad came to the phone. He said he and Mom would come out, to get everything ready, and that he would make sure Mom came.

A few days before they arrived, I got my acceptance letter at NAU, and, to my surprise, they accepted me directly into fourth year. I had to promise to do a ten-thousand-word thesis by the end of the year, though. Some humanities degrees allow you to do a thesis instead of some courses. I leaped at the opportunity to transfer what I had been working on in Chicago—they even gave me a scholarship.

Aunt G drove down to pick up my parents in Phoenix. Becca and I would meet them for dinner at Aunt Gillian's after work.

"Are you nervous?" I asked Becca, as we got into her car to drive to—and I still couldn't believe it—our place so that we could change from our work uniform. I'd only been living with her for about a week at this point. Moving in was super easy. I had packed my suitcase from Aunt Gillian's house and unpacked it in the bedroom of our new apartment. I couldn't believe it was only six months since I had come to Flagstaff; I felt like a new person, like I'd gone from being a teenager to an adult.

"I was going to ask you the same thing," Becca smiled at me, leaning over for a kiss as she started the car. "But, yeah, I am. I mean... they're your parents. Meeting the parents is kind of a huge deal."

"Yeah. I'm nervous, too," I confided.

Becca said, "Don't worry, it will all work out—have some faith."

She was right.

We pulled up in front of Aunt G's house and made our way up the steps. My dad crushed me with a hug as we entered; he loves to squeeze during hugs. He was at least two inches taller than me and looked like a bear, with a gray and black beard and longish hair. My mom had once said he was a hippie who'd never grown out of it—he just covered it up with suits and ponytails when needed.

"Dad... Can't... Breathe..." I stammered.

"I've missed you, kid," he said, smiling. "And you must be Rebecca. It's a pleasure to meet you."

"It's nice to meet you too, Mr. van Wilde," Becca said, extending her hand. My dad, however, would have none of it. He swooped her into an enormous hug, Becca laughing the whole time. I noticed with a mixture of jealousy and relief that he did not squeeze her like he had squeezed me.

"Jeremy!" I heard Mom calling from the living room. I moved further into the house and saw my mom sitting with Aunt Gillian on the couch. My mom looked like Aunt Gillian, but older, and with hair that had half gone gray. I sometimes wondered if I had caused that.

"Hi, Mom," I said, bending down to give her a hug.

"Mrs. van Wilde," Becca said, coming behind me to shake her hand. "I'm Rebecca Weisen. It's nice to meet you at last."

"Hello Rebecca," Mom said, a hint of frost in her voice.

"Why don't you kids sit next to Lu on the love seat?" said Aunt Gillian.

I shot my mom a glare and turned to follow Becca to the couch. I sat down beside the cat, who lay straddling the arm. Lu blinked up at me before jumping on me, curling up in my lap. I stroked her head and ran my hand over the long gray fur of her back; she purred, which helped me to stay calm.

"Tea, Jeremy, and coffee for the rest of us," Aunt Sam came in from the kitchen carrying a tray filled with cups and pastries.

"Thanks, Aunt Sam."

"So, Becca," Dad started, "what brings someone from the land down under all the way up here where it snows all the time?"

Becca laughed and smiled. "Well, would you believe that while I was at uni in Melbourne, we had this newly minted PhD come down and give a guest lecture all about exoplanets? She was passionate and really sucked me into her talk about the discoveries she was making and the unique types of planets she could discover. I said I would study with her someday. I followed her career, and when I got into grad school, I sent her a letter—kind of a fan letter, actually. But she answered, and we became pen pals. Then, when I got my master's, she encouraged me to apply here at NAU so I could study with her."

Becca and Aunt Gillian both smiled at each other.

"Don't sell yourself short," Aunt G said. "You had literally the best proposal we saw here. And I will tell everyone because I know you won't," Gillian turned to Mom and Dad. "Rebecca got published—all on her own. No co-author."

My mom gasped. "Really?" Mom had been an academic, too; she studied geology before deciding to go into real estate after her master's program, so she would have more time at home with her kids. "Wow," she continued, "that is so remarkable. Well done, Rebecca." Mom smiled at her, and I felt the tension begin to drain away. I always knew Dad would love Becca, but Mom could be frosty to my friends, and I was worried about how she would react to my first girlfriend.

Over dinner, Mom and Becca talked non-stop about academics here and in Australia. Both vented over the publish-or-perish cycle and writing grant proposals. By the end of dinner, they seemed like they had been friends for years. Dad winked at me and whispered, "You did well to find her—now treat her like the partner and friend she is, and you'll be set," as we cleared the table and did the dishes.

My parents only had a few days to visit, so Becca and I showed them the Grand Canyon and the Meteor Crater outside town. I took them on a tour of the Observatory, and Aunt G took us all to some restricted access telescopes that even I hadn't seen before. Becca and I showed them Mars through the Clark telescope on one of our evening observations. We also took them for a walk around the university campus. Mom insisted on seeing the hospital and finding out more about their cancer clinic, much to my embarrassment. Becca took it in stride, telling me she wanted to know too, just in case. They finished their trip with a tour of our apartment; I tried to reassure Mom I was fine, and that we weren't living in squalor. When I finally drove them down to Phoenix for their flight back to Chicago, my mom gave me a hug as my dad unloaded the suitcases from the back of Becca's car.

"Jeremy, I am so glad you found Rebecca. She is a wonderful person, and seeing you two together... It's just melting my heart. You are so good for each other," Mom gushed.

"Try not to mess this up. Don't forget that if you break up with her, we're keeping her and dumping you," Dad added, coming around the back of the car with the bags.

"I'll add that to the book of advice I don't need," I said with a smile. It relieved me that they had come around about me staying out here. I mean—I was an adult now, so they couldn't stop me, but it was always easier when everyone in the family approved.

"Seriously, Jeremy," Mom said, "you and Becca have something special. I can tell by the way you each light up when the other walks into the room. The way she orients herself to be near you, and you her. It's like a modern fairy tale."

"But with fewer dragons and more consequences," Dad said, handing me a gift-wrapped box.

"What is this?" I asked. Mom gave Dad a confused look.

"I'd like to know that too..." she said.

"I'll tell you later." Dad wrapped an arm around her. "Open it with Becca when you get home."

"Jeremy, make sure you book your PET scan. I hate to nag you, but you know you have to do it—so please do it. You'll feel better when you do. I'm so glad I took the time to inspect the clinic at the hospital, it seems like they should be able to handle anything that comes up."

"No need to nag him, he's an adult capable of managing his own life," Dad reminded her.

I hugged him and Mom and waved goodbye as they walked into the terminal.

When I got home, I told Becca what Mom had said about her lighting up when around me, which made her smile, and we opened the box—it was condoms. My Dad the joker, ladies and gentlemen. Becca cracked up at the note Dad had left on the inside of the lid.

"Condoms prevent unintended minivans. Love a Dad, who is way too young to be a grandfather."

Becca took the strips of condoms to the bathroom and put them in the drawer under the sink. I was about to throw the box of Magnums (because my dad thinks he's a comedian) into the recycling bin when I saw another note scrawled on the bottom of the box. 'Jeremy, look in your sock drawer,' it said. I went over to the dresser and pulled out the drawer; inside was a second small box. I opened it and saw my grandmother's old pendant; sapphire, with ruby and diamond accents and shaped like a flower on a gold chain. I didn't know my dad had got it after she died. A note attached to the pendant, this time from my grandmother, read,

"Jeremy, this is for the girl who will become your wife. I wish that I could have met her. I hope she wears it at your wedding. Love from Grandma Lynn."

I had a rather large frog in the throat after that. When Becca, seeing me with moist eyes, asked what was going on as she came back to our bedroom, I replied "nothing" and that I was fine. I excused myself to get a glass of water. While out of the room, I stashed the box with the pendant somewhere safe, intending to give it to Becca in the future. I don't know why my dad had given it to me so soon— Becca and I had only been dating for a few months. Things were moving so fast, and it was outstanding, but marriage was an enormous commitment, and I wanted to be sure I was ready before making that leap.

Becca and I turned what would have been her sister's room into an office, which we joked was the study, and soon enough, it looked like a war zone. Two desks sat on either side of the room, and posters and charts hung on the walls. I tried to keep my desk neat, but after a few months, it looked like a paper volcano had erupted. Becca didn't even try, leaving books and charts all over her side of the room. Her whiteboard was awash in diagrams and algorithms that made my eyes water. We also had a small closed-in balcony, which we dubbed the conservatory. I made jokes about putting candlesticks and rope in it, just in case a colonel came to visit. The reference and the joke flew right over Becca's head, so I went out and got a copy of the board game CLUE at goodwill, and it became a quick favorite. Our living room had a small extension toward the front door, which was just big enough for a shoe mat—so, naturally, we called it the front porch.

Becca had a double bed and awful flower-printed sheets.

"I didn't know you were a seventy-year-old grandmother," I said when I turned to show them to her after finding them in the box she had labeled 'bedroom.'

"What, you don't like flowers?" she asked, looking up from another box she had been sorting through, trying to find her pajamas. We hadn't yet finished unpacking.

"I like flowers fine. I find it kind of funny that I'll be sleeping on the same style sheets my grandfather died in, though,"

The next day, I bought us an extra sheet set.

After we finished giving funny names to our small slice of heaven, we settled down, and, sure enough, school slammed us like a steamroller.

6

It surprised me how good the crisp September morning fall air felt as I walked to school for the first day. I hadn't expected things to cool off so quickly, but given our elevation and that there was snow on the ground in May, I shouldn't have been surprised. It was still warm in the afternoons, so I had brought shorts with me in case my jeans were too hot by the afternoon. The day began with an orientation session, filling out a bunch of forms in the office, and a guided tour of the school. There were a lot of science programs here I had never even considered, like Forestry—there wasn't much of a need for one in Chicago.

It thrilled me to be invited to join the very exclusive history program at the University of Northern Arizona. I felt how lucky I was as I took the new student tour. There was a bunch of freshmen and me. One place on the tour was the library; I marveled at the size of the history, languages, and literature section. I had been worried that because it was mostly a science school, the selection would be small; I needn't have fretted.

After lunch, each department broke up for a quick tour of classes and meetings with professors. The history department had about ten other new students and me. We sat around a meeting room table, and the head of the program met with us, telling us about the professors and their work. I knew most of this from researching the school, but getting to ask questions directly to the faculty made me feel sure I would like it here. What's not to like about being one of 25 students in my class versus one of thousands in Chicago? I liked the home town, where everyone knew everyone and the department's first-name basis atmosphere.

At the end of the day, I stopped by the school's medical clinic to meet my new doctor. I told her about my cancer history, and she had me do bloodwork. She told me I would have to get regular blood tests, but that for now, I could avoid the PET scan; we would book one if I showed signs of cancer. She gave me a phone number to call to arrange monthly bloodwork. I promised myself I would book the appointments once I was sure what my schedule would be. I was happy to avoid another PET scan—not that they were painful or anything, but the fewer tests, the better. I was feeling happy and excited; I finally knew what direction my life would take for the foreseeable future, and it promised to be good.

After school and the doctor's, I went home for a quick meal before meeting up with Becca at Lowell to work a stargazing night. I recognized some freshmen from the history department and gave them a special tour. I took them to see some telescopes that were typically closed to the public, and we all had a great time.

At the end of the night, Becca and I closed down the Clark telescope and afterward headed home. Then we broke the bed. Yep—we made love so hard we broke the bed.

After spending an hour after midnight fixing it, we fell asleep; the blush of our laughter and love-making still showing on our cheeks.

One day after another, I got used to being back in school. As days turned to weeks, Becca and I fell into the routine that people who love each other fall into when they wonder if they might want to spend the rest of their lives together.

And the slip of paper with the phone number for blood-work slipped deeper and deeper into my backpack without being remembered or found.

Between school and work, by the time mid-terms came around, I was so ready for a break. Turns out, Becca had a surprise for me, which was good, because I had one for her, too.

Becca made me promise to be ready, with an overnight bag packed, as soon as she finished her classes. I expected to be ready but became lost in my work until I heard the door open.

"Jer... Come on! Time to go!" Becca called out from the front porch. "We still have a long way to go, and we only have a weekend!"

I looked up guiltily from a paper I had been working on.

"Three seconds!" I called back, slapping the lid of my laptop closed and throwing it and my notes into my bag before sprinting from the study. I grabbed my small duffel bag I had placed earlier by the front door, and we were out of the house thirty seconds later.

"So, love, are you going to tell me where we're are going finally?" I asked, giving Becca a hug.

She looked over at me and smiled sneakily. She teased, "So many questions—you must be a history student."

"Pftt. Says the astronomer!"

"Touché," she said, and we broke out laughing as Becca drove out of town, heading west into the setting sun. We chatted as we drove, heading farther and farther west.

"Oh my god!" I called out, noticing a sign on the side of the road about three hours into the trip. "I have to see this! It's the Hoover Dam! I've never seen it before!"

Becca pulled off the road and down the access ramp. We made it down to the Dam as the last rays of the sun hit the canyon wall on the opposite side. Becca and I walked across the Dam hand-in-hand; she had never seen it either. As we finished our walk and headed back to her car, I pulled her in close. Her eyes crinkled as she smiled up at me. Our lips touched, and it felt like the first time—as it always did when we touched.

"I can't count the things I want to do to you," Becca whispered, desire in her eyes. She smiled at me in lust. "Let's get where we're going."

"About that…"

"You'll know in a bit," she tossed over her shoulder as she opened the car door. I ran around to the other side and jumped in.

We drove away, holding hands. To the west, a glow in the sky became brighter.

It was Vegas. We went to Vegas for the weekend. It's cliché, but neither of us had ever been. By the time we got there, it was dark—at least in the sky. We drove to the hotel up the strip, which was lit up so you would think it was daylight. We had to duck around the back to park, but there was no issue. We checked in, and they upgraded the room, the lady behind the counter telling us we looked cute. She also signed us up for the Players Club, so if we played or bought anything at the hotel, or half of the others on the strip, we would get points. Neither of us much cared, other than when she also gave us the Players Club discount on our hotel room. We waved goodbye and gave her a good tip before heading up to our room. We were up in one of the towers that looked down over the pool, which had a classical Roman bath theme. We enjoyed the view from the window for a few moments and then closed the curtain.

I unpacked in three seconds. Clothes from my duffel bag went straight into the dresser; my laptop went from the laptop bag to the desk. Becca unpacked almost as quickly; she had claimed the coffee table by the window as her workspace.

"I'll take a quick shower, can you get some ice?" she asked as she undressed.

"But the view...." I said, smiling at her with my back to the window. I got up and grabbed the ice bucket.

"Oh, come on, nothing you haven't seen before. And you'll see it again soon—I promise," she winked.

"Well then, I better get back fast," I replied, shooting out the door. When I returned, the bathroom door was closed, and I could hear Becca's voice echoing; she loved singing in the shower, and I loved listening. I smiled as I recognized the song she sang, "I go to Rio" by Peter Allen. I'd never heard of him before, but you can't live with an Aussie without picking up some of their culture.

"When my baby, when my baby smiles at me, I go to Rio..." she sang as I put the ice bucket down next to glasses with paper lids on the dresser.

I popped an ice cube into my mouth, enjoying the cold and slow trickle of water down my throat. I sat down to wrap up work on my paper. I had popped in another cube when Becca came out of the shower, a towel wrapped around her. I swooped down and stole a kiss. The cold from my mouth on her warm lips made her eyes shoot open.

"Shit Jer, why are your lips so cold?"

I opened my mouth and showed her the ice cube. I smiled when she looked confused.

"Are you eating ice?" she asked.

"Yes," I mumbled around the ice in my mouth, swallowing the cube. I felt its cold going down my throat and into my stomach.

I headed into the bathroom and stripped down. As I pulled off my socks, I locked eyes with myself in the mirror. I thought back to the last time when I had really looked at myself; it was the day before I met Becca, on my first night in Flagstaff.

Looking at myself now, I couldn't see any outward sign of how I had changed. I mean, I was older and much more tanned than I had been, but in a way, it made the scars from the past stand out more. And I mean literal scars from the surgeries for my cancer treatment. I looked at the one on my forearm. I idly thought about what I wanted as a tattoo to cover it one day. I'd been saying I wanted a tattoo there for ages. I thought I wanted something healing, meaningful, and fun. I was about to step over to the shower when I took a second look at myself. I saw the subtle ways I had changed. I had put on some weight for one; some muscles had become defined, particularly on my legs. Maybe I distracted myself and only saw what I thought, and I still thought of myself as having cancer. I shrugged and stepped over to the shower's glass door. I was just rinsing the shampoo from my hair when the door opened, and Becca walked in. She came over and looked me up and down. She licked her lips, dropped her towel, and got in the shower with me.

I greeted her with a low "Hey. Need another shower already?"

"Hey yourself, handsome. I've got something else in mind," she said, standing on tiptoes to kiss me. She put one hand on my shoulder, and the other found its way to my penis, which immediately became hard. I pulled her close to me, the water running down our bodies as we kissed. I reached down between her legs and the warmth radiated to meet my fingers as they began rubbing her clit and playing around her opening. She looked up at me with her big beautiful brown eyes and smiled. I grabbed her by the thighs and lifted her so that we were eye-to-eye, and I pinned her back against the wall of the shower. The stream of water hit me square in the back as I dropped her a few inches, engulfing my penis inside her body. She let out a gasp at the sudden penetration and began rocking her hips as I thrust into her over and over. My thumb kept playing with her clit. The warmth and wetness around my penis and the humid atmosphere of the shower made us both start sweating almost immediately. I saw the embers of passion in Becca's eyes roar into flame as she climaxed. As she peaked, her vagina clamped down onto me, and I began to cum. Within minutes, it was all over.

As I lowered her, some of my cum fell out of her and on to the floor. I slipped in it a little, only narrowly catching myself before I fell over. Becca immediately burst into gales of laughter. Her amusement had me laughing, and we spent the next few minutes giggling and washing the sweat and other products of our love-making off each other.

"Fun start to the trip, isn't it, Jer?" she asked with a grin as she made one of those towel turbans around her hair that I could never figure out how to do.

"Yeah, I dunno," I teased. "Maybe it would have been better if I hadn't almost FALLEN TO MY DEATH in the shower!"

"Haha, comedian," she quoted back to me with a wink and a kiss as she skipped from the bathroom to go change.

We took a quick walk through the casino and out onto the strip. We walked up and down the strip for a few blocks, taking in the crowds, lights, and activity all around us. The perfume of the flowers and the smell of cigars and cigarettes mixed into a distinct smell. Horns blared from the bumper-to-bumper traffic on the strip. After only half an hour, we started yawning; it wasn't long until we both needed to go to bed. So we did; king-sized beds are awesome.

We slept in late, relaxing in each other's arms. My belly was rumbling when I opened my eyes and saw Becca looking back at me, smiling.

"What?" I asked.

"You're pretty, is all," she said.

I smiled back.

She reached behind her and grabbed a pillow, gently hitting my shoulder.

"Time to get up, lazybones."

A quick shower, shave, and then I dressed to go out for the day. I stood looking down at the pool through our window, feeling the air conditioning hitting me in the face while waiting for Becca to get ready. I was getting cold from the air conditioning when Becca came up to me, spun me around with one hand, and reached up to kiss me.

"I have a surprise for you," she said.

"What?"

"Remember when we were out camping in the summer? You told me about how you wanted to get a tattoo over your arm?"

"Yeah. Weird, I was just thinking about that yesterday."

"Well..." She pulled a package from behind her back and handed it to me; it was wrapped in old sky charts.

"What is this?" I asked.

"Open it, silly!" she said.

I ripped off the paper and saw the back of what seemed like a gift card. I turned it around and saw 'Las Vegas Tattoo - Gift of 1 hour of Tattoo time' written on the front of the card. I looked up to see Becca looking at me nervously. She started to ramble.

"I know you were talking about getting a tattoo, and I thought it would be fun if I could be there with you when you get it. I have a sketch for a tattoo you might like that I can show you. I hope it's okay that I got this for you. I know…"

I cut her off with a kiss. Our tongues danced together as I held her close to me.

"I love you," I said.

"So it's okay?" she asked.

"I can't wait to get it," I said, "and I'd love for you to be with me when I do. What design did you come up with?"

She showed me a drawing of some lines and shapes over a backdrop of stars and galaxies. She said that it spelled out "I am Star stuff" in amino acids, which are the building blocks of life on earth. Beneath the amino acids was the phrase "Mi Estas Skribite En La Steloj," which means 'I am written in the stars' in Esperanto.

"It's perfect," I said back to her. "God, I have such a huge crush on you."

And it *was* perfect because it seemed like she and I were written in the stars.

"Well, I made a tentative appointment for tonight, if you want to go get it for sure," she smiled.

"Let's do it," I said, pecking her cheek.

Later that day, as we prepared to head out, I slipped my surprise for her in my jacket pocket. I had thought long and hard about my surprise and spent a lot of money on it. My aunts had helped me to decide on it and had even contributed to making it even nicer than I could have afforded on my own. Being poor and a student seem to go hand-in-hand these days.

When we got to the tattoo shop, they had me sign several forms. The shop was brighter than I expected, with pictures of art and tattoos on the wall. It smelled like industrial-strength cleaner, which made me feel more confident. Music played, and I could hear the tattoo guns buzzing.

An hour and several thousand questions for the tattooist later, I had fresh ink covering up my scar. Becca had asked the tattooist questions about the process, and soon enough, I had joined in—it helped to mask the pain. When they say that getting tattooed is like getting scratched, they're sure not kidding. Most scratches don't last for an hour, though. Our artist was efficient, and the tattoo flew across my skin. I looked at it under the plastic wrap bandage they had put on to keep it clean, and it thrilled me; it turned out even better than I could have hoped.

We walked from the tattoo place back up the strip and toward the hotel. When we got to the Bellagio, the water fountains were starting their show, so we stopped to watch. *Now or never*, I thought once the show had ended. I felt nervous, so I took a deep breath and said, "Becca?"

"Yeah?"

"I love the surprise you got me. It's fantastic. I.... Well... I have a surprise for you, too. I hope it's okay."

I reached into my pocket and pulled out an envelope, handing it to her with a slight tremble. A puzzled look came over her as she opened it and read the papers inside. Then she looked up at me in shock, tears welling up.

"Jeremy, I..." she stammered as the tears fell down her cheeks. I reached out to her and cupped her face in my hands, my thumbs wiping her tears away.

"Is this for real?" she asked, her voice hoarse with emotion.

"Yeah, it is."

"We're going home?"

I smiled at her.

"Yes, we're going. I checked your schedule and booked the flights according to your end-of-term exams and marking. And, of course, I cleared it with Aunt G."

My aunt was still technically Becca's boss—at least until she got her PhD, even if she was very hands-off in supervising her day-to-day work at school and on the telescopes.

When my Aunt Gillian and Aunt Sam found out that I had booked tickets for us to go to Australia, they damn near lost their minds. They gushed about how romantic I was and how cute it would be for Becca and me to travel and for me to meet her family. Aunt Gillian grabbed the reservation that I had made from my hand and was on her cellphone before I could even register what she had done.

"Yes, hello?" she had said, "I'm calling about a reservation that I made. I would like to upgrade to First Class," she said, putting on a pair of reading glasses.

"Aunt G! What are you doing?" I whispered loudly.

"Shut up, I'm making this even better," she whispered back, her hand blocking the microphone. "Yes, for Jeremy and Rebecca.... No... Yes, that's fine, I will pay for it... One minute for the credit card."

"Aunt Sam, are you really...?" I started.

"Jeremy, shut up—let us do this for you," My normally mild-mannered and even-keeled aunt whispered, the most mischievous smile stretching from ear to ear.

"Yeah, Jer. Listen to Sam," Aunt Gillian whispered.

"But really, I can't..." I started, trying to grab the paperback.

"Jeremy, if you don't let us do this for you, I swear I will never let you forget it," Aunt Gillian whispered. "Yes," she said in a normal voice into the phone, "you can bill that on my AMEX."

And that's how I was browbeaten into letting my aunts pay for our upgrade.

"But First Class? However did you...?" Becca stammered again until I once again cut her off with a kiss.

"I bought the tickets, Aunt G and Sam paid for the upgrade. And I won't ruin Aunt G's story about how they pressured me into letting them pay for that. I'm sure she can't wait to tell you; it's exactly her kind of story."

Becca laughed, the tears still flowing. Since she worked with my aunt, she knew EXACTLY what kind of story I was talking about.

"Jer, this is... too much," she said.

"Is it not okay?" I asked, my stomach falling.

"I love you. I can't believe I have someone in my life who would do this with me, who would pay for my flights home. But, I can't be this much in your debt. I'll think of a way to repay you," she said.

"I don't need you to repay me," I said. "I love you—that's enough for me."

"I know you do. Jeremy, when one partner in a relationship does something... well, something like this for their partner... it puts an unfair power balance in the relationship. So, I'll match this—somehow," she said.

"Really, it's no big deal," I said.

She kissed me.

"Jer, listen to me on this one. You did something deep and meaningful for me by giving me a chance to go home. And your Aunts spent a ton of money on this, too. So I *will* find a way to do something for you guys. I know you expect nothing in return for this, but it will make me feel better about it because this is such an enormous gift."

"Okay," I said finally, a little baffled.

"Okay," she said. "This is a super special, Jeremy. I love you so much. I can't believe I have a boyfriend who would do this for me."

My heart swelled.

I joked, "I can't believe I have a girlfriend at all."

She laughed with only a hint of ironic pity. We walked back to the hotel together hand-in-hand, both a little tired from the emotion of the day and one of us with a sore arm. Not long after we got back to the hotel, we fell asleep in each other's arms again, with Becca falling asleep first. As I watched her sleep, I wondered how I could be so lucky. I still felt the passionate sexual attraction I had felt for her from the minute I saw her. I felt a deep and profound love, too; the kind that made me want to rip open my chest and show my glowing heart to everyone. As her chest rose and fell slowly with her breath, I wondered at the beauty of her; the soft curves of her face; the slim body she kept in excellent shape; the warmth she made me feel. When she looked at me, it was like there was no one else in the world. I wanted to keep feeling this way for the rest of my life.

I pictured us retired, hair gray, sitting on a cruise ship, in a cottage, sailing on our own sailboat, or just enjoying tea on our front porch. I thought about what it would be like to travel to Australia with her. Maybe we would see a kangaroo, go to an opera at the Opera House, or dive on the reef. I pictured Becca in her swimsuit, and then I pictured taking it off her, and I smiled as I dozed off, lost in my fantasy.

Our time in Vegas was over so quickly, and then we were back at school. Becca had a calendar of Hubble Space Telescope pictures she kept on the wall of our kitchen. We would see it every time we went to the sink to do dishes or make food. As soon as we got home, she wrote in the number of days until we set out to Australia. She would tick off another day on our calendar each night before we went to bed.

Before we knew it, it was exams, and the two of us barely had time to sleep and eat. We struggled through our exam workload and paper writing, distracted by the thought of what was to come.

I was excited about our upcoming trip, though Becca had warned me about her mother.

"My mum can be off-putting to strangers. She may say things or ask questions that you might not think are appropriate. She has trust issues and is a bit unstable. Please keep it in mind. If she says stuff, she probably doesn't mean it, but either way, I'm on your side. I mean, I love my mom, but loving her means accepting her quirks and her baggage."

"Um, okay, thanks," I said, bewildered.

"Just keep it in mind when you're thinking about your expectations," she said.

I imagined beaches. I imagined all the sights of Australia that I had seen in popular culture. Sights like the Opera House, kangaroos, the Outback, koalas, and blue water-covered reefs. I tried like hell NOT to imagine sharks, snakes, spiders, and perhaps the scariest of all, the Aussie men with mullets and short shorts. Aussies called them Bogans, or so Becca claimed. She then had to explain that Bogan was slang for what we would call a hick or redneck in America.

Then our exams were finally over. We threw some clothes into duffel bags and made sure we packed shorts, swimsuits, and lots of sunscreen. Since the original flights I booked were the cheapest possible, we had to wake up stupid early for our flight from Flagstaff down to Phoenix. From there we would go in the wrong direction, to New York. After a few hours there, we would head back west to Los Angeles and finally over to Sydney. It had promised to be a miserably interminable day, especially with backtracking all over the continent, but hey—it was cheap. Now that my Aunts had booked us onto First Class, I was looking forward to all the flying. Becca was especially excited since she had never been to New York; even though we wouldn't leave the airport, she would still get to see the city from the window.

"I don't think it counts as being in a city if you don't leave the airport," I told her.

"We'll agree to disagree on that one," she said with a smile.

7

It was pitch dark when our alarm went off at 3 AM. I almost didn't wake up until Becca shook my shoulder.

"Wake up, Jer, time to get moving," she said, not completely awake herself.

"Uggh," I groaned, my brain starting to boot up. Then the memory of what we were about to do bubbled from my subconscious and into my brain. I just about hit the ceiling from jumping out of bed so quickly.

"STRAYA!" I shouted in excitement, using the slang term for the country.

"Straya, indeed," Becca said with a grin.

We each showered and threw on our traveling clothes, grabbing our bags. Then we waited for the Taxi. And Waited. And waited.

"Jer, we're going to be late," Becca said nervously, as I frantically tried to get through to the taxi company with no luck. In a bit of a panic, I called my Aunts. Luckily, Sam was coming home from her night shift at the hospital, and she swung by and grabbed us and took us to the airport. After a quick hug goodbye, we rushed through bag drop and the theater that is airport security. We made it to the plane just as they were making the last boarding call. We wouldn't have made it if Flagstaff hadn't been such a small airport, with only one flight at that time of day.

There was a small first-class cabin in the little regional jet that we took to Phoenix. Only about half an hour after take-off, we were back on the ground. Since it was such a quick flight, neither of us slept. The only service was a small glass of water before we touched down. We ran from gate to gate in Phoenix before getting on our larger plane to New York. When we boarded, we had the first two seats on the right-hand side of the plane, with Becca taking the window seat. The flight attendant soon came around with refreshments. I grabbed a water and Becca an OJ, all the while holding my hand.

"Is this your honeymoon?" the flight attendant asked with a smile.

Becca and I traded a look. I smiled at her and started to reply, "no," when Becca squeezed my hand and nodded, saying, "Yes."

I raised an eyebrow at her, and she smiled back at me.

"Well then, I know it's a bit early, but we will have to break out the champagne!" the flight attendant said with an even bigger smile. "Congratulations!"

He opened the champagne in the front galley.

"Becca, what are you doing?" I whispered, leaning over to her.

"Well, we've been living together for six months in a committed relationship," she whispered back. "So we could say we are common-law married. And since this is our first big trip after that six-month date, we can call it a honeymoon if it gets us free champagne."

"Becca, you know we get free champagne anyway because we're in first class, right?" I whispered back with a chuckle.

"Um... Yeah, I totally knew that," she fibbed. Her face flushed a little.

"God, you're adorable," I said with a smile.

"Good, because if we are going to get married someday, I want it to be more official than we just happened to be living together," she said, giving me a light punch on the shoulder.

We chuckled. We had discussed marriage and kids early in our relationship, and while we had both decided that we didn't want any, we did want to get married someday. We even agreed that either of us could propose when we felt ready because we were equal partners in this relationship. Other people, AKA my mom, thought this was a bit weird, but we didn't care because it worked for us.

During the four hour flight up to New York, and after several glasses of champagne, Becca got some sleep. I, as usual, found it challenging to sleep on the plane, so I dozed and read my book. I reached over and woke Becca up so she could see the Manhattan skyline come into view from our window. We wound around the city for a while before finally landing at JFK. We chatted as we took the interterminal transfer over to Terminal 8. Once there, we got to use the lounge, eating delicious food and drinking even more champagne before heading down to the plane that would take us back to LA. This time, it was a jumbo jet, with a giant kangaroo on the tail; QANTAS, the national airline of Australia, few this flight through LA to Brisbane since the range was too far for a non-stop flight. In LA, passengers could connect to other QANTAS flights. When we got on the plane, the flight attendant checked our boarding passes and showed us to our seats, saying "Welcome home" to Becca in a full-on Australian accent, which sounded both familiar and completely different.

"Thanks," said Becca, tears beginning to well again.

"Are you okay?" I asked.

"It's been so long since I've been home—like, four or five years now. I don't know. It's just emotional for me to hear our accent again from someone other than my family. And the thought that I'm heading home again... Thank you for this, Jer," she said, leaning over for a kiss.

This flight, even though longer, seemed to go by much faster. We set our seats into bed mode and relaxed, drinking Australian wine and holding hands in silence. Becca fell asleep for a while, resting her head against my arm. It seemed like no time before we were on the ground in LA and transferring to the airplane that would take us to Sydney. This one was a full double-decker, with four engines and a massive wing. When we got on board, they gave us even more champagne and a little kit full of lip balm, soap, a toothbrush, and other stuff. A set of slippers lay at our seats for us to wear, along with a set of PJs we could keep. At this point, it would be fair to say that I was drunk, and Becca was also tipsy.

The engines were quieter than I had expected, and soon we were lifting off and heading across the Pacific Ocean. When we climbed higher, the seatbelt sign turned off, and Becca and I took turns heading to the washroom to change into the PJs. The food was fantastic, and the wine was flowing. Once that was all over, we folded our seats into beds, and they brought us an extra pillow and a duvet; soon, we were both sleeping.

I woke up to Becca's quiet laughter about five hours from landing. It was still dark outside and in the cabin. She was watching a TV show I didn't recognize. Becca, seeing that I was awake, leaned over and whispered, "Hey, I have an idea."

She grabbed my hand and pulled me to the back of the top deck.

"What are you..."

"Shhh," she whispered, pulling me into a washroom.

As the door started to close, a flight attendant saw us, winked, and held his finger to his lips. I smiled and nodded.

Joining the mile-high club was awkward. The washroom we were in was bigger than one you would find in economy, but it was still small. Becca got down on her knees, and after doing away with my pants, took me into her mouth. Her tongue worked magic on me as I sighed, leaning back on the sink and closing my eyes. After a few seconds, I was hard and ready to go. I pulled Becca up, and we traded spots with her leaning over the sink. I pulled down her sweatpants and entered her from behind.

I don't know much about sex, but every time seemed to feel better than the last. The taboo of doing this in a public space at 38000 feet made me even more excited. I was cumming in her in no time. Since she hadn't gotten off yet, I flipped her so that she sat on the sink and went to work on her with my tongue. She was moaning in no time, and I shot my hand up to cover her mouth to muffle the sound. She dug her fingernails into the back of my neck as she climaxed. We cleaned up a bit and snuck back to our seats.

"I can't believe we did that," Becca said.

I smiled at her, and I'm sure it was as dopey a smile as ever.

Soon, the sun rose on the other side of the cabin. The cabin's lights came on, and the flight attendants served breakfast.

Then the coastline came into sight. From that point on, the view glued Becca to the window. The plane turned and followed the coast northward for some time before turning over the coastline and the suburbs of North Sydney. We turned again, and soon, the Opera House and Harbour Bridge came into view, with downtown Sydney behind them. We got lower and lower, and I grew more and more excited. Finally, we were over the runway and then on the ground. The airplane finally came to the gate. The flight attendants thanked us for flying with them as we got off the plane, the heat of the Aussie morning hitting us through the jetway. Customs formalities completed, including an Australian passport stamp for me and another "Welcome home" for Becca, and we were officially in Australia.

Becca led the way to the train downtown. We were staying at a new hostel in an area called The Rocks. We got off the train at Circular Quay, the famous Opera House, and, dominating the skyline, was the famous Sydney Harbour Bridge. A bunch of ferry docks appeared right in front of us, and to the left was a cruise ship tied up alongside the harbor wall. Buskers played the didgeridoo, and the smells of food wafted from the cafe patio outside. Announcements notifying passengers of departures to places like "Paramatta" and "Manley." The first thing I did was take a bunch of selfies, as you do, and even got a laughing Becca in some of them. We walked up to our hostel, which was halfway up the hill toward the bridge. It sat over top of an archeological dig. I checked us in, and when we got into our private room, we saw that we had a fantastic view of the Opera House outside our window.

"Wow, this is incredible; I can't believe we're here," I said.

"I know," Becca said. "Let's go for a walk."

We left the hostel and walked down to the water. The first thing we did was get local SIM cards for our phones so we could make calls, text, and use the Internet while here. I texted our selfies at Circular Quay to Aunt Sam and Aunt Gillan, with a note thanking them again for the first-class upgrade.

I almost got on the wrong escalator at the mall. Becca grabbed me before I tripped and reminded me that foot and vehicle traffic were on the opposite side from what I was used to. It was neat listening to Australians talking with their accent and realizing that to them, I'm the one with the accent.

We walked around the Opera House and through the botanical garden. For lunch, we ate meat pies, a traditional Aussie dish that we got from a food truck. They were delicious, and I wondered why we didn't have them back in the USA. After an hour or two of walking around Sydney, Becca suggested we go to a beach. It sounded like an outstanding idea to me. We had agreed we couldn't nap, as it would only make the jet-lag worse.

We jumped on the ferry over to Manley, a suburb at the entrance to Sydney Harbour. We enjoyed the rest of the afternoon on the beach and swimming in the warm ocean. The sun was warm and bright, and the salty smell of the ocean permeated the air with each crashing wave against the beach. Becca looked so beautiful as she frolicked in the waves. Her smile was radiant, and her skin glowed as it got some much-needed sun. Throughout the day, her accent grew thicker and thicker until she spoke like the born and bred Australian she was. By the time we took the ferry into town, the sun had almost set. The city was lit up, and the sails of the opera house glowed white against a dark blue background as the ferry pulled into Circular Quay.

We got back to the hostel and showered. When Becca came out all done up in towels, I unwrapped her like a Christmas present. I took in her beauty as she stood there, naked.

"My goodness, how did I ever get the most beautiful girl in the world to agree to date me?" I said.

She smiled at me and started pulling my clothes off, too. Soon, we were both naked, and I pulled her onto the bed. I kissed her, and when she opened her mouth to allow our tongues to touch, I reached down and started playing with her clit. I didn't waste any time getting my face down there, aside from a quick stop to kiss and nibble her small breasts. My tongue lapped at her clit and worked its way inside her lips, which opened up like a tulip flower blooming. Her juices coated my chin as she climaxed, encouraged by my tongue and my fingers dancing on her breasts. As she crested, she pulled at my hair, holding my face against her mound. She let me up for air after a few seconds, and I crawled back up over her. As I kissed her, I penetrated her deeply. She let out a gasp at the sudden fullness and opened her legs wider for me to have deeper access. I thrust slowly and gently at first, and then built up speed. It felt like I could feel each ridge and ripple of her vagina as it expanded to fit me. I tried to not go too deeply into her since, I had learned, if I thrust too deep too hard, it really hurt her; so I was as careful as I could be before burying myself as deeply into her as I could go without hurting her, as I exploded inside her. We lay there like that for a while, with me growing soft, just making out. She flipped me onto my back, moving with me so that I was still inside her, and she laid on my chest. We just breathed. When my penis finally popped out of her, I could feel a dribble of cum mixed with her fluids fall out onto my pubic hair. We smiled at each other and fell asleep.

We spent the next day touring Sydney. We visited the museums and got a backstage tour of the Opera House. An opera would be playing that night, and since our tickets gave us a discount, we figured 'what the hell' and got tickets for it. Becca and I both love music, and the opera didn't disappoint. We saw La Bohème; it was my first opera, and while I didn't understand what they were saying, the costumes, sets, lighting, and music helped get the point across. A screen above the stage also translated what they were singing into English, and I guess that helped, too.

The next day, we took the train over to Melbourne. It was a beautiful journey, and we got to see the countryside go by from the train window. Becca wanted to show me where she had completed her undergrad, and we met up with her friends from school.

We spent the day riding around the trollies with Becca's friends. They visited old haunts and museums that I was told I couldn't miss, but we never found the time to go into. We happened to be there during a street art festival, and we were up half the night looking at the art exhibits and installations covering the city's buildings. You could play Tic-Tac-Toe on an office tower using buttons on a pedestal down the street, and lights and stands opened all over. We didn't get to bed until well after midnight.

The next day, we got to explore on our own. We went to the Royal Victoria Museum and saw a wonderful exhibit about Aboriginal culture—Beth would have loved it. We stopped at a sports outfitter store, and I bought an Australian Outback hat, which I learned was really called an Akubra. That night, we went bar hopping, just the two of us, and had a blast.

A few days later, we were to fly up to Alice Springs so I could finally meet Becca's family. At 2 AM the day we traveled, I woke to hear her throwing up in the bathroom. I got up and went to the door, asking, "You okay?"

"I'm fine, Jeremy, go back to bed," her words muffled, her head still in the toilet.

"Can I get you water or anything?"

"I said I'm fine. Please leave me alone." She looked up at me, and I saw puffy red eyes and pale cheeks that made me even more worried, but her glare had me turn and leave, as she had asked.

The next morning, we woke and had breakfast as if nothing had happened, but I could tell there was still something wrong. I hoped it wasn't serious, and that she would feel better soon.

Throughout the flight north into the center of the country, the land became redder and redder; all I could see from the window of the airplane was a road running through the red emptiness. Every half hour or so, a tiny village drifted past, lost in the landscape of sand and dried out lakes and rivers. Before the plane touched down, the pilot said it would be 46 degrees on the ground.

"115 degrees to you," Becca told me, "and you really need to learn how to use a real temperature scale, Jeremy." She winked at me but didn't smile.

When we got off of the plane and walked across the tarmac, the heat took my breath away; I could now understand why the hat I wore had such a large brim.

"Ah, it's a bit chilly today," Becca said idly. I followed her down a tree-lined path, breathing in the fumes from the jet fuel as we made our way toward the hopefully air-conditioned terminal. The closer we got to Alice Springs, the moodier and more distracted she seemed to become. I took the opening and made a joke, trying to make her smile.

"Yeah, I wish I packed my parka. Around what time does the snow start?" I said.

She turned back, and, seeing the sweat dripping from my face, she laughed.

"At least it's not humid," she said, stopping. She waited for me to catch up and took my hand with a squeeze as we stepped inside the terminal.

Becca's sister picked us up from the airport.

"Hi, Abby!" Becca squealed as she saw her sister.

"Heya, Becks," Abby replied with a grin as the sisters hugged. "I'm not used to seeing you so often. And this must be lover boy. Damn, you're cute, even in that silly hat," she looked me up and down. "I know you were there when I was out in the USA, but I never had time to meet you. Wish you had met me first." She licked her lips and glanced at Becca in envy.

"Hi, I'm Jeremy," I said, offering my hand.

"Nah, Lover Boy suits you better," Abby said with a grin. She pulled me into a hug and, to my surprise, gave me a kiss on the cheek.

"Abbs, don't be an ass," Becca said to her sister, punching her in the arm and grabbing my hand possessively.

"But it's true," Abby said with a laugh and a wink at me. Becca looked at me over her shoulder, and I smiled and laughed, but squeezed her hand reassuringly.

The sisters got into the front seat of what I was later told was a Ute, but to me was a pickup truck. I piled into the back after tossing our bags into the bed of the truck, and we headed out of town. The two sisters chatted, and I joined in every once in a while, but I mostly looked out at the Outback scenery.

I was nervous about meeting Becca's mom, especially after what Becca had said about her earlier. Other than that, though, I didn't know much about Becca's family other than her sister. Becca rarely spoke about her mom, and she never talked about her dad. All I knew about him was that he was estranged from his family and was in jail for some crime. Becca didn't mention what, and I didn't ask.

It took three hours to get to their farm. The rumble of the tires over the road became a low drone, and the sound of the AC blasting full cold filled the truck. The family owned a vast sheep farm, or station, as they call it in Australia, by a place called King's Canyon.

When we got there, Becca's mom stood outside on the porch waiting for us. I could hear sheep bleating in the distance, and the air smelled of sweet grass and sunshine. Becca ran into her arms, and they hugged for a long time, alternating between laughing and crying. I grabbed our bags from the back of the Ute and carried them up behind her.

"And you must be Jeremy," Becca's mom said as she turned toward me, an arm over Becca's shoulder.

"Yes, ma'am," I said, immediately going into super-polite mode, which is a kind of my default when I'm nervous. I dropped our bags and took a step forward, offering my hand, which she accepted. Instead of shaking it though, she pulled me into a bear hug; it surprised me how tightly she squeezed for such a small woman. Her hug reminded me of the kind my Dad gave.

"None of that 'ma'am' nonsense—you can call me mum, or Gwen," she said firmly.

"Yes, ma'am—I mean, Gwen. Thank you very much for letting me stay with you," I said.

"No worries at all," Gwen replied. "I have to look after Becca's man. Welcome to 'straya. I wish you guys could have stayed longer than the week you'll be here; I've got lots of stuff planned for you and Becca."

"Mum, seriously, we don't need to do a big production," Becca said, as Abby came up behind her and grinned at the three of us.

"Nonsense. This is your first time in Australia, right, Jeremy?"

"Yes—actually, it's only my second or third time out of the USA. We did family trips into Canada a few times when I was a kid. I never ended up going anywhere else until now."

"Well then, Becca, be sure to show him around. And I have arranged for some things for the two of you as well."

"You didn't have to do that," Becca said.

"I wanted to, Rebecca—I'm happy to have my daughter back in my home, even if it is only for a week, and I'm happy she finally has a serious man in her life," Gwen said.

"Um, thanks," I said.

"Mum, it's soooo hot; can't we go inside? Becca and Lover Boy might turn into a puddle if they stay outside much longer," Abby complained, smiling.

"Yes, lets—we can give *Jeremy* the full tour," Gwen replied, shooting a glare at Abby, who just shrugged and smiled.

The house had a modern and airy feel, with a kitchen and dining area when you walked in. Further back was an enormous office, and off to the right was a living room. Upstairs had four bedrooms and a bathroom. There was also air conditioning, which was very welcome.

We settled in a guest room. Abby told me later that none of the bedrooms upstairs were the same as when Becca was growing up; they had renovated the entire house when she was 17, and none of it was the same as the one before. They even moved the bathrooms.

After unpacking, we went back downstairs to watch the sunset on the front porch. We had some beers while Abby worked the barbecue. Gwen asked me about myself; she wanted to know when my birthday was, about growing up in Chicago, about the cancer—a lot about the cancer, actually, including my recovery. She also wanted to know how Becca and I met. When Becca protested that she already knew, Gwen replied that she wanted to hear it from me, so I re-told the story, including my crazy aunts, how we went camping, and how we came here. I left out all the sex, though.

"Okay then, my last question... for now. Yes, I have more questions, Becca," Gwen said, overriding Becca's protests.

"What would you like to know?" I asked. I was reeling a little from all the questions.

"How long have you been in love with Becca?"

Abby laughed. "Jeremy and Becca sitting in a tree," she sang under her breath, but loud enough for us to hear.

"Shut up, Abby!" Becca shouted, annoyed.

"Well, I know it's cliché, but I fell for her when I first saw her at the Lowell. But—and I know this sounds crazy—I fall even deeper each time I see her. I'm not a poet, but this is the most genuine thing that has ever happened to me," I said. I looked over at Becca to be sure I hadn't said too much; to my relief, she smiled, leaned in, and kissed me.

"Well, okay then," Gwen said.

"Dinner time!" Abby called out.

We had some meat I had never tried before; it was tough and had a strange taste, but I liked it a lot. I found out later that it was kangaroo tail. I didn't even know that you could eat kangaroo. As the sun went down, the stars came out. Becca took me for a walk down one of the roads on the farm, carrying a blanket. We walked out under millions of stars, clearer than anywhere I had ever been. The moon set not long after the sun, and we were in one of the darkest darks I had been in. It was even darker than Beth's campsite, where Becca and I had spent the night when we first started dating. It was quiet. Through the darkness, you could only hear the occasional sheep and dogs barking, but other than that, it was still; there wasn't even a breeze to rustle the grass.

Becca shook out the blanket and placed it on the side of a tiny hill. We laid down together and held hands under the stars.

"Sorry about my mum, she can be a bit overbearing," Becca said after a while.

"It's not a problem; I don't mind answering questions. Your mom's not as scary as I worried she would be."

She rolled onto her side to look at me.

"What did I do to get a guy like you?" she asked.

"You were yourself? I dunno, I ask myself the same thing every day," I said. "Only what I've done to get a woman, not a guy."

"Would you say that no matter what happened? Would you stick by me if you found out that I had done something terrible? What if I needed you to look after me because I couldn't walk or move?" Becca asked.

I used my elbows to prop myself up and turned to her.

"Would you stick by me if the cancer comes back?" I asked. "You would have to do something horrific to get me to stop loving you. A minor thing like being sick wouldn't stop me."

"Yeah, I would be there for you if the cancer came back," she replied quietly.

"Becca, I love you. I don't just lust for you, even though I of course find you wildly attractive," I said, rolling over on top of her and looking down into her eyes.

"As professions of love go, I give that one a four-point-five out of ten," she laughed, reaching up and pulling me down for a kiss. I felt relieved that the tension and withdrawal I had sensed in her this morning seemed to have vanished.

We laid there under the stars, listening to the sheep and feeling the scorching air blow over us before we finally went back to the house to go to bed. I couldn't sleep, so I went to the bathroom for some water. I saw myself in the mirror and remembered the last time I'd spent any proper time looking at myself back in Vegas. I noticed that ever since I got the tattoo, I hadn't thought of myself as a sick person. Not a cancer survivor, Just Jeremy. I smiled, then filled up and drank a cup of water, and went to bed again, finally drifting off.

Becca woke me before the sun rose the next morning.

"Get up, Jer. We're going to King's Canyon today. You have to see it since we're here. And if you want to do it and not die from the heat, you need to get moving now."

I got out of bed, and before I knew what was happening, we were in the Ute and driving. About fifteen minutes later, we pulled into the parking lot; the first part of the hike was the worst.

"It's called Heart-attack Hill," Becca said. She pointed at the first section of the trail, which seemed to be hundreds of steps going straight up the side of a cliff. When I had asked if she was serious about climbing those steps, she laughed and bounded up them, with me trying to keep pace behind her. When we got to the top, we had to walk along a narrow ridge that had a steep drop on one side and the cliff wall on the other. Once we got over that, we were on top of the canyon. I was about ready to pass out, thinking that maybe I should have worked out more often. Becca gestured for me to follow her, but I held up a silent hand and sat down on a rock, panting while she chucked.

"When I was a girl, I used to come here all the time," Becca explained, sitting next to me. "The sunrise is beautiful up here, and you have to be out of here by seven or eight AM in the summer because they shut the park down—too many tourists getting heatstroke," she said. "Come on, walk, and you will feel better." She pulled me to my feet, and we set off down the trail.

"I would hike all over the canyon. I would jump in the pool in the Garden of Eden, even though we aren't allowed to, strictly speaking."

"What Garden of Eden?" I asked.

"Not what, *where*. And where is there," she said, pointing as we rounded a corner. A lush forest appeared at the bottom of the canyon. I could see tall green trees, flowing streams, and lots of wildlife.

"Wow," I said in awe.

"Yeah, I know, right?!" Becca said. "Just wait till we get down there."

Another half-hour on top of the canyon and a series of stairs down into the valley below brought us into the garden. Becca showed me the natural pool where she would swim as a child. It was the size of a big pond and sat where the stream ran through the canyon, making a hard right turn as it descended the gently sloping ground. Becca hushed me, listening as she seemed to make a decision.

"Hurry before the first tour groups show up," she said, stripping off her clothes and jumping naked into the pool of clear water. The sunlight penetrated the tall canopy of trees, highlighting the most beautiful parts of her body. Each of them glowed with the light, and none of them noticed until now. I grinned, and before my dick got too hard, I peeled off my sweaty clothes and jumped in after her.

We climbed back out as the first tour groups showed up; we only just got our clothes on in time. The rest of the hike was easier once we had climbed out of the canyon again since from there, it was all downhill back to the parking lot. When we finished the hike, Becca drove us back to Gwen's house.

Becca and I helped around the farm for the next few days, and she seemed to relax and enjoy being back home. By helping, I mean we carried hay and sheep feed around and drove through the fields on ATVs counting sheep. I was happy I had made this possible for her, and it was fun to play farmer for a bit, even if I felt like I was melting most of the time.

The next day, Gwen had an announcement.

"Well, everyone," she proclaimed, "we're going to Uluru tomorrow—I can't have a guest from so far away not see it. We're going to go after dinner. It's a four-hour drive down in the camper. We'll spend the night, and then we'll be up at the break of dawn for a walk around Uluru before it gets hot. And yes, Abby—that means you, too."

Abby groaned and rolled her eyes. "Okay, Mum," she muttered.

"Good," Gwen said. Becca looked over at me; she smiled and squeezed my hand.

"You'll love it, Jeremy; dawn is the best time to see it. Oh, and Uluru used to be called Ayers Rock," Becca whispered, smiling as she saw understanding cross my face.

"Speak up, you two. If you're talking, then talk to everyone."

Becca repeated what she had whispered to me.

"Good," Gwen replied. "Just because you don't live here anymore, Rebecca, doesn't mean that the rules have changed," she chided, but with a smile.

"Yes, Mum," Becca said, turning to wink at me.

I smiled back at her tentatively. I still wasn't sure how to read Gwen. She was a bit intimidating, both because of her no-nonsense personality and the fact that I wanted to look good in front of her so that she would accept Becca and me. This was the first time I had ever met a girlfriend's parents, after all, and I still didn't know if I was doing it right.

"Let's go for a walk, Jeremy," Becca said.

"Be back in time for dinner, you two. That's in fifty minutes, in case you don't know," Gwen reminded us.

"We will, Mum," Becca said.

"See you soon," I said to Gwen and Abby.

Abby smiled and waved while Gwen nodded.

We walked out of the front door, across the porch, and down the steps to the driveway.

"There's a little trail to the fire pond that I loved to walk when I was younger," Becca said, as she led us out toward the road.

"What's a fire pond?"

"It's a pond with a pipe in it so that if there's a fire, the fire department can use the water. Think of it as a natural fire hydrant."

She took my hand and shielded her eyes as she looked around, although what she was looking for, I didn't know.

"Do you think your mom likes me?" I asked.

"Yeah, she likes you fine. I know it's odd to be around her sometimes. She starts off treating you like the prodigal son, but the more she likes you, the curter and more abrupt she is. She's been like that for a while."

"Have you been feeling better?" I asked. Becca had thrown up a couple more times since we got here.

"Yeah, I'm feeling better—I think it was just nerves," she replied.

"What do you have to be nervous about?" I asked.

"Well, it's been so long since I last lived here. I keep in touch with mum by phone or email, but we're not all that close anymore. I worried about what she would think I became since the last time she saw me. Don't get me wrong—I love my mum, but I sure didn't always. And I wanted her to like you."

"Would it have mattered at all if she didn't?" I asked.

Becca reached out and held my hand.

"Not at all, Jer. You're as much my family as Mum is, or even Abby, who I love and keep in touch with much more than the rest of them. It's cliché, but I love you more than there are stars in the sky."

"From an astronomer, that's high praise," I said, squeezing her hand and smiling.

We walked along the path by the pond, lapping it twice before heading back to the house for dinner. The next day, after we finished the afternoon chores, we made the long drive to the campsite in Ulara, the city next to Uluru national park. While Becca and I lit a fire outside, Abby and Gwen made up the three beds in the camper. We climbed up and stood on the roof to watch the red rock glow with the light of the setting sun before the canopy of stars emerged over us. Becca and I went for a quick walk under the stars before we crawled into the upper bunk and fell asleep. I was so tired I didn't even think about the fact that I was sharing a bed with Becca in front of her mom and sister—not that we got up to anything. I was asleep before my head hit the pillow.

Once again, it felt like almost no time before the alarm in the camper went off, and we pulled ourselves out of bed and drove down to the rock. I could barely see the outline against the faint light growing in the east. One of the weirdest things about being in Australia is that the sky is upside down. In Flagstaff, the sun rises somewhere in the east or southeast and moves across the southern sky before setting in the southwest; same thing with the moon and the planets. To see them, you usually have to look south. Not here; the sun rose in the northeast and moved across the northern sky. Also, the constellations were upside down. I had noticed it even before Becca pointed it out, which was an excellent sign that her astronomy lessons were sticking, and that I was at least competent in my job as a guide at an observatory with public star nights.

Becca and I had planned to walk together, separate from Gwen and Abby, but Gwen had other plans.

"Becca, you will walk with me; I want some mother-daughter time. Jeremy, you can go with Abby—Becca and I will take the path toward the right, and you two can go left. The path goes right around the rock, so we'll meet back here whenever we finish. And we'll see you on the other side," Gwen announced.

I looked over at Becca, and she just nodded and smiled somewhat grimly at me.

"All right then, lover boy, you're with me today," Abby said, pulling my arm as we started walking left around the giant rock's base.

The gravel of the walking track mashed under our feet as we set off side by side around the rock.

"Becca is lucky," Abby said after a while.

"How do you mean?" I asked.

"To have you. I'd love to meet someone like you. You're funny and hot. Does Becca say that to you often? Do you have a brother?"

"No, I have twin sisters," I said, dodging the first question.

"Well, damn. I was hoping you could set me up."

"Why didn't you come to school with us?" I asked.

"Well, for one thing, someone needed to stay home and keep an eye on Mum. She's not always totally stable—

emotional abuse does that to you sometimes, you know."

The rock glowed red with a shimmering light from the east.

"Is that what happened? Becca hasn't told me," I said.

"If she hasn't told you, then I better not till she does."

Fair enough, I thought, wondering again at what the secret was that Becca kept. First, Aunt Sam mentioned some sort of dark past, then Becca's change in mood as we came here, and now Abby. I guessed it had to do with her father, whom she never mentioned, but I didn't quite understand what it was.

Abby and I continued to walk in silence. The sun continued to rise. The sky started an inky black, slowly turning purple and then orange and then blue. I kept looking at the rock, smooth in some parts, distorted in others. I can't deny I felt a primordial connection to the place. I looked over at Abby, who focused mostly on her shoes.

"Isn't this incredible?" I asked, trying to draw her back somewhat.

"It's okay, I've seen it," she replied, not looking up.

We walked for another while in silence again.

"Look, Jeremy, don't mind me. I just find it hard to keep secrets, and this is big. I think it's kind of bullshit that you've been dating Becca for so long, and she hasn't told you. You deserve to know if you plan to be with her, to protect her, to make sure nothing hurts her like that again. And if she loves you, she should be honest with you, and part of that is sharing everything. Yeah, maybe not right away, but for sure by the time you're living together. That's what I think. But like I said, it's her story," Abby said.

I remembered Becca saying that she was on my side with her family. I wanted to be on her side, too, so I said, "It's not a big deal to me. I don't need to know all her secrets. I trust she'll tell me when she's ready."

"Yeah... Sure," Abby said, shooting a glare past me. Down the track, I saw Gwen and Becca walking towards us.

Abby glared at Becca as she walked by. Becca saw and looked at me questioningly. I shrugged and made the 'I have no idea' face. Becca nodded. Once again, we walked in opposite directions, but now I wondered what this big secret was. The more I wondered, the more I promised myself I wouldn't ask; that I would live up to the commitment to be there for Becca when she was ready to tell me, and not to pry. But deep down, I also grew worried.

Abby walked the rest of the way in silence. I tried not to let her get me down and to enjoy the rest of the walk. It had turned into a beautiful morning, and it was getting uncomfortably hot when we all got back to the camper. Gwen and Abby jumped in, with Becca saying that she needed to use the washroom and grabbing my hand to go with her.

"What's going on with Abby?" Becca asked.

"You remember when I promised not to pry about the thing with your past when we were camping?"

"Yeah," she said, confused.

"Abby thinks you should have told me."

"Oh, she does, does she? After everything I did for..." Becca began to storm toward the camper.

I pulled on Becca's hand to stop her and spun her to face me; her face flushed with anger.

"Becca, please—I am on your side. I won't ask you to tell me; I won't say anything. I'm on your team, but I won't lie to you about why Abby is upset, even if I don't understand. My promise to you still stands."

"This is none of her business!" Becca said, fuming.

"Becca, I don't know what else I can do other than be here for you."

She slumped, sighed, and looked at me apologetically, the anger draining from her face.

"I'm sorry, love," she breathed. "It's been a rough day so far, walking with mum. And now to have to deal with Abby, too...it's almost too much. I'm happy you're here with me, and I'll tell you someday, but not today—I can't take it. I'm happy I got to see my family, but I'm super ready to be heading home in a couple of days."

I smiled at her. "I'm so happy I got to come, but I have to admit that home with just the two of us sounds really nice."

We walked back to the camper and grabbed the two seats in the very back, with Gwen and Abby up front. Becca dozed off, resting her head on my shoulder. I wasn't far behind, my head on hers, and still holding her hand. When we finally got back to the farm, everyone took the rest of the day off since it was too hot; Gwen told everyone we could unpack the camper tomorrow.

The next morning, everyone was up early. Before breakfast, Becca and I unpacked the camper while Gwen checked the mail, and Abby put away food and washed dishes.

I was carrying in the last load of dishes from the camper when I heard something smash in the kitchen, and Gwen shouting in rage. Soon after, Becca stormed from the house —absolute fury on her face.

8

"Becca!" I called out in alarm. "Hey, wait up."

I ran into the house and put the dishes on the front porch. I turned to run after Becca when Gwen grabbed my arm, holding me back.

"Let her have some time, Jeremy. Please, please let her go for a while," she said.

"What's going on?" I turned to face her.

"We got an official letter from the government that my ex-husband—Becca and Abby's father—was released from prison early. Good behavior, so they say. This is most unwelcome news for us all, but especially for poor Becca. It's dredged up some nasty memories, and it's unfortunate that she got it here, of all places. It's probably best if you two get away from here as quickly as you can. You can take the Ute. Text us where you leave it, and I will have one of the farm staff fly out and pick it up. But she can't stay here—she can hardly stand being in this house anyway, and this will make it impossible."

"What the hell happened?" I asked Gwen.

"That isn't important right now, Jeremy!" She held up a hand and regained her composure. "I'm sorry. What happened doesn't matter. What does matter is what you can do to help Becca. I don't want to see her be hurt more than she already is, and the best way to do that is to please take her and go. Go down to Adelaide and visit the wine country. Go do silly touristy stuff you had planned to do before flying home. Becca had always wanted to visit the Barossa—take her. You guys had planned to leave from Adelaide in a couple of days, right? Well, I'll cancel your flights for you from Alice Springs to Adelaide if you can get going now."

"Yeah, we are leaving from Adelaide. This is so weird. But, okay, I'll do it."

"Good. Abby, go get their things and get them down here, please. Jeremy, do you think you can drive here?"

"Yes, I think I'll be okay driving." Driving on the wrong side of the road had tripped me up at first, but now it almost felt natural since we had spent so much time doing it recently.

"Good. Here are the keys. Adelaide is a sixteen-hour drive, so if you leave now, you should get there around one AM." Gwen tossed the keys to me. Abby ran down the stairs with our bags and handed them to me.

"Well, it's been... uh," I said awkwardly.

"I wish your visit had ended under better circumstances. I hope we will see you again when things have changed. I have a lot of legal things to deal with. Go after her and get her away from here." Gwen gave me a hug goodbye. Abby shook my hand. I left, tossing our bags in the back of the truck and jumping into the right-hand seat. I started the truck and headed down the driveway and onto the road, where I could see Becca in the distance. I drove behind her, pulling beside her and rolling down the window.

"Want to run away together?" I asked, trying to lighten the mood.

Becca turned to me, her face one of abject despair mixed with complete fiery rage. My heart broke seeing her like this. She climbed in the truck, and I started driving. I reached out for her hand, but she pulled it away. I immediately moved it away from her and just drove. I was sure she wasn't mad at me for anything, and that she needed some space, so I pressed on in silence, not even listening to the radio. After an hour or so, we pulled onto the main road heading south towards Adelaide. A few hours later, Becca finally spoke to me.

"Thank you, Jeremy—for coming to get me, and for getting me out of there."

My heart screamed at me to comfort her, to reach out somehow and show her how much I loved her, but all I could say was, "You're welcome, Becca."

I looked over at her; tears continued to fall down her face. I reached into the back of the truck and grabbed one of the water bottles I knew was back there. She took it from me with a nod, but careful to make sure she didn't touch my fingers.

We continued to drive down the road, nothing but bush and the occasional roadkill kangaroo. I kept driving. Eventually, the sun set. I kept driving. Becca kept to herself, huddled against the opposite side of the Ute. And we kept going. Soon, the stars came out. I grew tired near Port Augusta and pulled off into a parking lot to sleep for a few hours.

It was early morning by the time we reached Adelaide. I pulled into the hostel that Google suggested as a good place to stay when I had made reservations at a bathroom stop earlier in the day.

"I'll check us in," I said, climbing out of the Ute. I left the keys on the front seat. "Come in when you're ready. If you aren't when I have keys for us, I'll come back out and let you know what room we're in and leave a key for you." She looked at me and nodded.

I checked us in, being sure to ask for two beds in our room. I didn't know what was going on with her, but from the way she acted in the car, I figured she might need space. I dropped our bags off in the room and then walked back out to the Ute. Becca hadn't moved.

"We're in room 202. I got separate beds, just in case you need some space. I'll see you up there when you're ready." I closed my door and turned to walk back up to the hostel, then I heard the other door open. Becca got out, locking the Ute and walking up beside me. Together, we walked in.

Our room had bunk beds and a queen bed. I got into the smaller bottom bunk, with Becca taking the queen-sized bed closer to the bathroom. Soon, I fell asleep. Becca woke me by tossing and turning in her bed a few times. Around four AM, she got up and came over to my bed, crawling in beside me. I slid back to the wall, and she pressed herself against me, finally getting some sleep.

We woke around seven.

"I'm sorry, Jer," Becca said, turning toward me.

"Don't be," I said. "I'm on your team, through good times and bad. I don't know what I can do to help, but let me know, and I'll do it."

"Thanks, love. Let's do something fun today. I want to forget about yesterday, and today is our last full day in Australia—let's make it count," she said.

We walked down the stairs to the reception area to see if any tours were available for the day. We were lucky enough to jump on a tour of the Barossa Valley, as Gwen had suggested.

"I always loved the wine from the Barossa," Becca said, with the beginning of a smile.

I loved the Barossa tour, but I was still concerned about Becca; she seemed to be lost in her thoughts sometimes, and she still didn't hold my hand. I was worried for her. We tasted some superb wine and ate some wonderful food, and all the while, Becca seemed to be almost back to her old self. But as soon as it was over, she became withdrawn again. The tour ended, and we drove back to the hostel. That night, again, Becca tossed and turned and moaned in her sleep, keeping me awake until again she came over and climbed in with me. I wasn't sure if she wanted me to hold her. I was dozing off with my arm between us when she reached over and pulled my arm around her like a blanket, tucking it across her chest and holding onto it. The next morning, my arm was fully asleep, which woke me up. Becca still slept, so I lay there for a few minutes before my arm hurt too much, and I moved it.

"Good morning, Jer," Becca said, not turning to face me; she was awake already.

"Hi, Becca," I replied.

"I'm sorry," she said again. "It's been rough, but you've been so great to me. I want you to know that I appreciate that. I know that the problems I have right now are not your fault, and I love you so much for giving me space. I'm working on remembering that I choose to let you touch me."

"Let me know if you want me to do or not do something," I said.

"I will," she replied. It had been three days since we had held hands or kissed; we hadn't had sex since we arrived at her mother's house. I didn't mind, but I noticed it because it was so different from usual.

We showered, getting dressed in the bathroom—a marked difference from how we usually acted around each other. Becca threw up again on the day we left. Try as I might, I couldn't help but miss how we used to be. I wondered if we would ever be like that again.

We went for a walk in one of Adelaide's many parks. I could smell the flowers and the grass, and a warm breeze rustled the leaves. We ate lunch at a small cafe and then headed back to the hostel to get our bags and leave for the airport. Becca was quiet all morning; I didn't force a conversation.

The airport smelled sterile, and the inaudible hum of announcements filtered through the check-in hall. I ran down to the arrivals level before we checked in and dropped the keys to the Ute off with one of Gwen's staff, who had flown down that day.

Becca and I checked in for our return flight, and once through security, we went to the lounge. We waited there and had some wine until our flight to Sydney was called. Becca drank more than I expected. I worried for her. She and I were the first ones on the airplane and the first ones off again in Sydney. We got our transfer over to the international terminal and went through immigration and security. We waited in the lounge for our flight to Dallas. When we boarded, we had barely said five words to each other since we had left Adelaide, spending the time in silence. It wasn't the 'silent treatment' though, more like the silence you get when two people are reading. When the wheels lifted off from Australia for the long trek over the Pacific, Becca reached out and held my hand. I looked over at her; she was crying again.

"I miss Australia. It's still... home to me," she said.

I also felt sad to be leaving Australia because, on the whole, it had been a great trip; the ending was disastrous, though.

"Maybe we can come back sometime if you like—in the future, I mean. And maybe if we... if we're together for a while, we can move here or something."

She smiled back at me.

"I love you, Jeremy," she said, a hint of a sob in her voice.

Twenty hours later, we were back home in Flagstaff in the cold. We still had a few days before classes started back up. Becca remained subdued from her usual happy self. We began taking walks every evening before bed. The temperatures were frigid, especially compared to Australia, reaching into the minus four range. The night before term started, they forecast a blizzard.

The snow started falling at noon, and the temperature warmed as it did. Soon, two feet of snow lay on the ground, and it was still falling. I had shoveled the snow in front of our apartment twice by seven PM. The snow made a satisfying crunch as I stepped on it, and the smell of the cold filled my nose.

When I got back in, I called out to Becca. "Do you still want to go for a walk tonight?"

She came out of the bedroom, almost dressed for our walk.

"Yeah, let's do it." She walked over and slipped into her boots and her jacket. We stepped together out into the snow and turned left at the bottom of the driveway, walking east towards Mars Hill a couple of blocks away. When we got into the forest at the bottom of the hill and started walking up the trail, Becca grabbed my hand.

I looked over at her and smiled. She looked up at me.

"Jeremy, there's something about me I think you deserve to know."

"What is it?" I asked.

"It's about Dad, and what happened to my family when I was sixteen." She brushed off a bench along the track, but we didn't sit down.

"Okay," I said.

Then the words tumbled from her.

9

"When I was fourteen, my father started drinking, and when he drank, he started getting touchy with women. First, it was only a beer or two with the boys at the pub, and then it became more and more. I don't know why he started, but when he did, it wouldn't stop. I had just finished puberty at the time, and when he drank at home, I was the one he would start with.

"It was innocent at first, or so I thought—a hand on the shoulder or arm; a pat on the back. But then it got worse. A pat on the back became a caress. The more he drank, the braver he got. Soon, he was unclipping my bra through my sweater. I told mum about it, and she didn't believe me. She said there was no way my father would unhook my bra because it just wasn't done. Then she punished me for lying.

"It kept going on like that until I finally stopped telling her. And that's when my dad moved on. It was three days after my eighteenth birthday. I was almost finished high school and looking forward to the freedom of university that fall when it finally happened. Hands started going under shirts, and up thighs and into pants. My father was the first one to touch my breasts. He was the first to stick a finger inside me. It hurt, and I cried, but that just made him laugh. I tried to hide from him, but it didn't work. One day, I ran away, and he found me out in a field. There was no one around. That's when he finally did it."

Her voice became detached and cold—almost clinical, as if she were reading from a textbook. She looked toward the ground, and the words came steadily, but with no emotion.

"He pushed me down to the ground saying, 'well, there's the naughty girl, running away from home and her poor ol' Dad.' And then he pulled out his knife and cut my shirt open, popping off all the buttons. He grabbed my breasts and squeezed them; the alcohol on his breath damn near made me throw up. I turned my face so that the sun silhouetted him, so I wouldn't have to look at him. With a sudden movement, he pulled down my pants and forced my legs apart. Before I knew it, he was on top of me, fiddling with his belt and holding me by the throat with the other hand. I didn't know what was happening, but the next thing I knew, he was between my legs, and my vagina felt like he had thrust a knife into it. He moved in me with violence and alcohol-induced rage. He called me names. He continued to rape me until he couldn't hold it back anymore. He came inside me. He left me there, black and blue, dripping blood and semen. He was the first person to be inside me, Jeremy."

She looked up with a tear, her voice catching on my name. Where she had just spoken with no emotion, now a flood of feelings came out.

"And it didn't stop there. It kept going and going, week after week until I got pregnant. When he found out, he took me behind my mother's back into Alice Springs and got me an abortion. He told them someone from high school had knocked me up. We came home with a warning about unprotected sex and that I would need a few days to recover. But he still didn't stop. Soon, I stopped crying and resisting him. By then, it was summer, and I was counting the days left before I could get out of there. But that made him madder. When he saw me counting down the days, he started beating me. And then he stopped even that because it wasn't fun for him anymore. And he had a new target —Abby.

"It started slow for her too, the same way, with innocent-seeming touches. But I knew what would happen next, especially when I left in a few weeks. I knew I couldn't let what happened to me happen to her, so I set him up. I dressed as sexy as I could, and when Mum was off on a shopping trip into town, I started feeding dad alcohol. I knew my mum would be back in a few hours; she had intended to spend the night in Alice because it's such a long drive. I made sure she would come back because, as she was leaving, I stole her wallet from her purse; she wouldn't have any money or credit cards or anything. And when my dad started getting touchy, I made sure it was me he was interested in instead of Abby. So I sent her outside to do chores and took him to my parents' bedroom.

"When my mother came back, she walked in on him, with him still inside me, and me crying and him hitting me. She believed me then. The police arrested him that same day. Mum felt ashamed that he cheated on her, ashamed that she hadn't believed me, and horrified at what had happened without her noticing. It broke her. It took until I left to come to the USA before she would look me in the eyes. He was my first. Isn't your first supposed to be about love and teenaged innocence? He did everything to me. And the worst part of it all, I had to seduce him, to welcome him into me, inside of me, to get it to stop. And then I had to tell this story over and over. To my mother, the police, the lawyers, the judge and jury and courtroom, but I did it. I did it because I couldn't let it happen to someone else—especially not to Abby."

She looked back up at me and saw the tears in my eyes.

"Oh god..." I leaned forward, my stomach aching, and my heart breaking. I wanted to throw up, but I didn't want her to feel worse than she did, so I tried to keep it together.

"Oh god," she echoed, gasping for air. "How can you ever want to be with me again, knowing who was in me before you? Knowing that I was pregnant with his parasite?"

I reached toward her, and she took a step back. I held up my hand and let it drop, showing her I wouldn't touch her if she didn't want me to.

"Becca, I'm so..."

"Don't be sorry!" she cried, cutting me off. "It's not your fault—I should have told you sooner, but I didn't want you to be thinking about him when we were together. And I didn't want to think about him ever again, but how can I not, now that he's free? I choose to be with you. You have never made me feel like I don't have a choice, but now that you know... are you still going to want me?"

I held out my hand to her. I wanted her to know that nothing had changed. That I still loved her. That I still wanted her. That I marveled at how brave she had been to spare her sister and trick her father into getting caught. How much I wish that it had never happened. How much it sickened me that someone could do that to her. How much I wanted to just... hold her and save her from the demons of her past.

"I love you, Becca. I do. I want to do everything I can to make this memory go away. I chose you on the first day back at the observatory, and I still chose you."

Becca reached out and grabbed my hand. We both stood there, arms outstretched, holding hands, both of us crying. And then she pulled me close and embraced me, crying into my chest. She looked up at me with red cheeks, and I took off my glove and wiped a tear from her face. I don't know what she could see on my face, but I hoped it was clearer than my words had been.

We comforted each other in the snow. The evergreen trees strained under the weight of the snow they held. The wind swirled the falling flakes around us and the cold bit into our cheeks and ears. My nose was freezing. I felt a drip of snot fall from my nose and caught it with a hand. But it wasn't snot—it was blood. I watched with fascination as it poured onto the snow.

"Jeremy... You're bleeding."

10

BECCA DECIDED that she wanted to work with a counselor to deal with her dad being released from prison. She used the counseling service provided by our school. Even though we were almost on the opposite side of the world and there was no way he could get to her, he still terrified her. I supported her as best I could. Our sex life stopped for obvious reasons. The counselor wanted to see me, too. I wasn't sure why, but since Becca had asked me to go, I went without question.

The waiting room seemed almost sterile. It had a clean smell, like a doctor's waiting room. Instead of health posters on the bland walls, there were posters about mental health issues. There was no one else in the waiting room as I sat down. Some bland elevator music played over the speakers. The receptionist typed on her keyboard, and in the background, I could hear someone on the phone.

"Jeremy?" A kind voice asked.

I looked up and saw a woman who looked like she was in her 70s with white hair and a salmon-colored shirt and blue jeans. She stood at the door leading from the waiting room and into the offices.

"Yeah," I picked up my stuff and walked toward her.

"Welcome." She held the door open and led me down a modern hallway that had multiple doorways and into an office. Inside sat some comfortable-looking chairs and footrests.

"My name is April. Please, take a seat."

I sat down on one chair, and she sat across from me, kicking her feet up onto an ottoman between us. A salt lamp sat on her desk, and a floor lamp behind me; the rest of the lights in the room were off.

"Please make yourself comfortable."

Okaaaaay, I thought, leaning back in the chair a little.

"Have you ever been to counseling before?"

"Yes."

"Okay, good, so you should be familiar with how this will work," she said. "The first thing is that everything we discuss is 100% confidential. Rebecca won't know anything that you say here, and likewise, I will reveal nothing she has said. However, I am also a mandatory reporter. I am required by law to report if you show that you may harm yourself or others. Other than that, though, nothing will leave this room. I will take notes, but this is mostly so I can remember what we talk about."

"Okay."

"So, tell me—how have things been going with Rebecca recently?"

"Well, I gave her a trip home to Australia as a gift, and while we were there, she found out they released her father from prison. She never told me what he'd done, and when she found out he was free, it really hurt her. I tried to distract her until she got home, but for the first day, she barely spoke and wouldn't eat. I tried to give her space, got two beds in our hostel room, even though we hadn't slept apart since we moved in together. She tried sleeping in the other bed, but after having what seemed like nightmares, she ended up sleeping in the same bed as me anyway. It took a while for her to come around, and she didn't tell me the entire story until we were back home."

"How did you feel when she told you?"

"Honestly? I felt sick. I almost threw up when she told me. And I felt angry."

"Who were you angry at?" she asked.

"Her father. That someone who should have loved and protected her violated her."

"And not at her?" April inquired.

"No! No, of course not—none of this was her fault. She did the best she could in a terrible situation."

"For not telling you?"

"Well... I wish she had told me before I took her to Australia. I'm not angry. I don't know if I would have been able to tell her if something like that had happened to me. I wish she had told me because then I might not have taken her into a situation where she might have to re-live what happened," I said firmly.

"Do you blame yourself for taking her home?"

"I... I felt guilty, even though my brain knows that's not rational. I had no way of knowing what had happened, right? I had no way of knowing that her dad would be released. But...my heart is telling me I took the person I love most in the world to a place where she was traumatized. And then she got hurt again while there, at a place I took her."

"Okay. So what's the first thing that comes to your mind when you think about it?"

Betrayal, I thought. I had taken her to a place where everyone had betrayed her. Her father. Her Mother. Me.

"I guess I'm worried she'll think I betrayed her like everyone else did there." I slouched down in the chair.

"Do you think she feels that?"

"I don't know—I hope not. But I can't help but be on eggshells a bit, waiting for the hammer to fall."

"Does what happened to her make you feel differently about her?"

"Yes. How can you not feel pity and regret that something that terrible happened to someone you love? But it hasn't changed anything. I'm still in love with her. I'm still attracted to her, and I still want her in my life for as long as she will have me."

We spent the rest of the appointment going over strategies to help me help Becca.

I drove home through the snow and found Becca waiting for me in our living room. She was reading a book but didn't seem to turn the pages.

"Hi, Becca," I said as I walked through the door.

"Hey," she said, distracted.

"How have you been?" I asked.

"Good. I'm not excited about term starting back up tomorrow."

"I know. Want to go out tonight?" I asked.

"I don't really feel like it, Jer," she said.

"Yeah, I figured as much," I said.

She looked up at me with hurt in her eyes.

"Which is why," I continued, turning to bring in a bag from the grocery store, "I got the fixings for a delightful meal at home tonight. I even made you an invitation."

With a deep bow, I handed her a card saying that I invited her to a formal dinner this evening at our house. Black tie or equivalent, as a joke since I knew full well that neither of us had clothing like that.

"Black tie?" She coughed, which might have been the seed of a laugh.

"Yes. This will be a very formal dinner—only the best is good enough for my girlfriend."

"Well, okay then. I accept." She hesitated. "... I'm sorry that I've been moody. I'm trying not to take things out on you." She walked over to me and stood on tiptoes to give me a kiss. "I love you, and I'm so grateful that you're the best boyfriend ever. I don't know what I'd do without you. How was your appointment?"

I smiled and gave her a hug. She stiffened and then relaxed into it, hugging me back with a squeeze. "It was fine. She asked some very uncomfortable questions that I didn't know I had been worrying about. So, on the whole, it's a good thing I'm going."

I started cooking and had the table nicely set with candles and everything when she appeared wearing a red dress.

"You look beautiful," I said.

"The tux looks good on you too." She nodded at the T-shirt with the print of a tuxedo and bow tie on it.

"Dinner is served, ma'am," I announced, taking her by the arm to her seat, which was marked with a name tag.

I served dinner, and she relaxed and chatted. After it was over, I brought out dessert and some port I had picked up at the Duty Free on the way home from Australia.

"I've been saving this for a special occasion; now seems about as good as any."

We sipped at the fortified wine with appreciation.

"Jeremy?"

"Yes?"

"Thanks for dinner."

"You're welcome, love."

She came over and sat in my lap, and we held each other for a while. She finally stirred and got up to clear the rest of the dishes. After clearing them, I turned on the stereo.

"May I have this dance?" I held out my hand. And we danced.

The school term started slowly, which gave Becca time to ease into it. Soon, she was pretty much back to normal, with a smile and a kiss every day—although we still hadn't had sex. It was fine; I knew she needed time and space; it didn't change the fact that I loved her. I could take care of myself. Spring break passed by in a blur. Soon, I was thinking about work for the summer. I was all set to graduate, and so was Becca. They had already accepted her to do postdoctoral work at the observatory—it was only natural that we would spend at least another summer working there.

Then it happened—we graduated. Becca had her graduation first. My aunts and I were in the front row when they called her name, and she walked across the stage in her gown and cap. We gave her a standing ovation, and she beamed at us. Well damn, I was in a relationship with an actual Doctor now. I couldn't have been more proud.

The next day, it was my turn, and when I walked across the stage, they were there in the front row for me. I grinned at them and winked at Becca. They handed me my scroll, and that was that. All that was left to do was figure out what I would do with the rest of my life. Simple, right?

That night, my aunts took us out for dinner to the nicest restaurant in town. We celebrated until the early hours. Becca and I crawled into our bed, barely having time to take off our clothes before we fell asleep. I woke up to Becca rubbing my back.

"Good morning, handsome," she said.

"'ello miss," I replied in a fake British accent.

She leaned over and kissed me, taking my hand and putting it on her breast. It was the first time in almost six months that I had touched her sexually.

"Are you sure?" I asked.

"Yes. I want to bring back the good feelings around sex and forget the bad ones."

I caressed her breast and played with her nipple before bending down and taking it into my mouth. I sucked and teased it and moved over to do likewise to the other side. Becca reached down and started playing with herself as I worked my way down. I kissed her breasts, then her abdomen and belly, and finally made my way down to her pubic bone. She took her hand and pulled me back up for a kiss, moving so I was between her legs.

"Just do it," she said, guiding me inside her.

The first penetration in so long caused me to last about fifteen seconds before I erupted in her. I kept kissing her and thrusting throughout, barely becoming soft before I was hard again. I flipped her over and pushed back in doggy style, reaching around to play with her breasts. I kissed her neck and shoulders as she pushed back with each thrust. She turned her head, and I leaned forward and kissed her.

Our tongues entwined as her vagina constricted. I could feel the beat of her heart as she clenched down on me in the throes of her orgasm. I came inside her again as the tremors of her pleasure washed through her body. We collapsed onto our sides and breathed heavily for what seemed like an eternity.

She rolled over and faced me. "You're bleeding again." She reached over, pulling a tissue from the box at the side of the bed and handing it to me.

"Thanks."

"You've been getting a lot of nosebleeds, Jer. Do you think maybe you should get that checked out?"

Ugh. I did not want to go to the doctor's office if I could help it; I'd had way too many unpleasant memories of doctor's offices in my life. Plus, I had the newly remembered guilt for having forgotten to book those blood tests so long ago. The realization that I had forgotten hit me hard.

"I'm sure it's only the dry air," I said, swapping tissues and hoping against hope I was right.

"Yeah, but they sure have been happening a lot recently..." I cut her off with a kiss before running to the bathroom to wash my face and stop the bleeding.

"Gross! You got it on me!" she shouted, following me. We took a shower together to wash off the blood. I wiped down her back, running my hands along the curves of her hips as she pressed back into me.

"Remember that night in Vegas?" she asked.

"Yeah. I remember almost dying," I said with a laugh.

Then we went to bed.

I tossed and turned for hours before I finally drifted off. I promised myself I wouldn't forget to book the tests again.

But, deep down, I knew I would.

And so I started grad school. I knew it would differ from undergrad, but I didn't understand how different it would be. I had TA duties, classes I had to take complete with papers to write, and my big thesis. Becca taught a few classes but had been invited to take part in a partnership between Lowell and the Naval Observatory, which was down the road from Flagstaff. They wanted her to continue her work in finding exoplanets, and she was doing other classified research for them too. I wouldn't understand it anyway, so it was no big deal for me.

After the first week of settling into the routine, my thesis advisor, Professor Jensen, asked to see me so we could discuss what I wanted to write about for my thesis.

"So, I know from your undergrad you were exploring ways that languages influence culture—specifically Esperanto and the global society of Esperanto speakers that emerged as the language developed," she said.

"Yes. I thought it was interesting to look into the social and historical roots of Esperanto and the people who speak it. Being detached for any one geographical area, how did the culture of Esperanto develop? Especially considering its start in the 19th century Europe, which was so nationalistic."

"Do you think you still want to work on this topic?"

"Actually, I was hoping to make it more multidisciplinary," I said. "I want to explore how language influences culture throughout history. For example, you can look at the schism in dialect between the French and Québécois, who arguably speak a more pure version of French than the French do. So a combination of history, linguistics, and anthropology."

"That could be interesting. Why don't you go ahead and draft up your proposal? Be sure to include the specific questions you want to answer, and I'll see you again in a month."

I agreed.

Becca and I settled back into our routine, and she got better and better. She started calling her mother and sister more and was relieved to find that her father was back in prison for parole violations. Apparently, the first thing he did when he got out of prison was to try to go back to the family home.

Gwen had prepared for this; she even had the local cop over for tea when he arrived. Since visiting his victims violated the terms of his release, the officer immediately put him in handcuffs and hauled him back to jail. It took no time at all for the court to remand him to serve out his full sentence in prison, which would be at least a decade more. When she got the news of the court's verdict, Becca was noticeably more herself. We laughed, and Beth had us work some evenings at public viewings. We regretted that neither of us had the time to work anything more than casually at the observatory anymore.

When Dr. Jansen approved my thesis proposal, Becca cooked dinner for us and invited my Aunts over to celebrate. Before we knew it, it was Thanksgiving, and the temperatures fell below freezing again.

Soon after, it was Becca's Birthday. I surprised her with a rose petal path to our bedroom when she finished work early in the morning. She came in to lit candles and more rose petals on the bed.

"What's all this?"

"Did you think I would forget?"

"Forget what?"

I laughed, "I think you forgot instead. Happy birthday, Rebecca."

She looked at her watch and, with an exasperated sigh, said, "Damn. Would you look at that?"

She grinned and dropped her bag on the low table at the foot of our bed. I got up and kissed her passionately. She looked up at me and smiled, reaching down to the bottom of her golf shirt uniform and pulling it over her head. She hadn't been wearing a bra today, and I bent down to kiss her neck, the hollow of her throat, and along each collarbone. I rubbed my hands up her belly and gently tickled her nipples before reaching around her and picking her up. I placed her on the bed and stripped off her pants and panties. I kissed her feet, and she spread her legs as I kissed my way up them. When I got to her clit, I wrote out her name on it, and before I knew it, she was pulling my hair, my head clenched between her legs. I smiled at the power I had to make her feel so good.

"Don't stop," she whispered, panting.

I kept going, running our names over her nub with my tongue, and she came again. This time, she pulled me up to her face, and as she kissed me, I slipped inside her. She was still clenched from her latest orgasm as I rocked inside her. She rolled us over and rode me hard. I reached up to her hips as she rocked and met my thrusts from above.

Before long, I was cumming inside her, and as the sun rose, we fell into a sweaty sleep under the covers, wrapped around each other.

We woke up in a sea of red—not from the red of the now-crushed flower petals, but from the crimson tide of blood pouring down my face, staining the sheets and our bodies.

11

I TRIED TO SIT UP, but my head spun; specks of light flooded my vision as I fell back on to the sopping pillow. I reached over to Becca and shook her but could barely move my arm. Luckily, she woke with a groan.

"What is it?" she turned to face me and immediately saw the blood.

"Oh my god, Jeremy, are you okay?"

"Can't... get up... dizzy..." I muttered with little strength.

"I'm calling 911."

"No... It's okay. I just... need to get to the bathroom to clean up."

I struggled to my feet and immediately fell to the floor, the blood continuing to trickle from my nose.

That was enough for Becca.

"Jeremy, try to relax. I'm calling for help," she said, pulling out her cellphone.

After she called 911, she grabbed a box of tissues, and with me still lying on my side on the floor, she tried to help get the bleeding under control. There was an awful amount of blood everywhere, or so it seemed to me. Becca's cheeks, usually rosy, were very pale, and her eyes gave away her panic. I could tell she was trying to keep her face controlled so as not to worry me.

I closed my eyes, feeling awful. I felt drained, coupled with a headache and the feeling that I was drowning in my own blood—which, as far as I knew, I might very well be doing. The only space my brain seemed to have was in the unpleasantness of drowning very slowly.

When the medics arrived, they lifted me onto a stretcher and rushed me to the ambulance. On the drive to the hospital, Becca held my hand as the medic started an IV and pushed some medicine to help my nose stop bleeding. I wouldn't let myself believe what I knew was likely to be true—the cancer was back.

When we got to the hospital, they wheeled me straight into the Emergency Department. Becca tried to follow me in, but someone stopped her to get a statement on what had happened.

They gave me a blood transfusion because they couldn't be sure how much I had lost. They ran a lot of tests, but I was feeling groggy, and then I had passed out. When I woke, they had filled my nostrils with cotton, saying that they had cauterized the bleeding in my nose. The grogginess had been from some drugs they gave me to relax so they could do the procedure.

"Where is Becca?"

"Is that the young lady who came in with you?" someone asked.

"Yeah. She's my girlfriend."

"Sorry, sir, next of kin only."

"But I live with her...."

"Sorry, sir—you're not married, so we can't let her in. You can see her during visiting hours. Do you have family we can call?"

I screamed internally. *'Becca is family!'* I breathed a few times. "You can call my aunt. Becca has her number."

They wheeled me upstairs to keep me overnight for observation; they wanted to be sure I didn't bleed again. When we got to the room upstairs, a nurse came in to introduce herself to me.

"Hi, Jeremy, I'm Claire—I will be your nurse this evening."

"Hi, Claire. Do they know what happened? Anything come up on my tests?"

"I'm not allowed to tell you the test results, but we have scheduled our hematologist to come in to talk to you when she starts her shift in a few hours. Try to get some sleep."

"Can I see Becca? My girlfriend? She came in with me."

"Sorry—hospital policy. We can't let her in outside visiting hours. I can pass on a message, though, if you like."

"Yeah, just let her know I'm sorry for wrecking the bed."

"Your Aunt Sam is here. Would you like to see her?"

I yawned, "Sure." I was so tired.

"Hey, Jeremy," Aunt Sam said, coming into the room in her hospital scrubs. "I was on break when Gillian called and said you were here. Are you okay?"

"Just a silly nosebleed."

"I can't look at your chart since I'm not your nurse, but if you need me to explain things or anything like that, then text me. If I'm sleeping, I'll have Gillian monitor my phone. Try to get some sleep. You're in excellent hands."

"Thanks, Aunt Sam," I said.

She nodded and slipped out, and I drifted back to sleep.

The next morning, a middle-aged lady walked into my room wearing a white lab coat, a purple stethoscope around her neck.

"Jeremy, hi, I'm Dr. Jones. How are you feeling this morning?"

"Better, but my nose hurts," I answered. Twenty minutes earlier, Nurse Claire had taken the cotton swabs from my nose. It still smarted from removing all that dried blood. "Do we know what's wrong with me?"

"Have you been feeling any fatigue or shortness of breath recently?" she asked. "Sweating at night? Getting sick more than usual?"

"Yeah, actually, I guess so," I replied. "I've been having all of that for a while now, but I thought it was some lingering cold I couldn't get rid of—nothing serious enough to come see a doctor about, though."

"Well, we did a bunch of blood tests last night, and you are very anemic."

Shit.

"I think it would be prudent, given your history, to run some more blood tests and get you scheduled in for a PET scan, some X-rays, and an abdominal ultrasound. Maybe a bone marrow biopsy, too, just to make sure we don't miss anything before we try to work out why you are anemic."

"Should I take some iron pills?" I asked.

"That won't be much help. Your iron levels are fine; you just don't have as many red blood cells as we would like to see."

"Okay, I guess we can do the tests. I've been NEC for a few years now, though." NEC means no evidence of cancer; it's the term they use instead of saying 'cured' because the bastard might actually come back.

"When was your last PET scan?" she asked.

"A while ago," I sighed.

"Well, you will want to do one anyway, to be sure you're still clear. You should do one once a year for the first few years, coupled with regular blood tests. If you're still NEC after two or three years, we will spread them out further; you want to catch any relapse quickly." She frowned, "And I can see here that last year your doctor tried to schedule you for monitoring blood tests. Why didn't you book the appointments?"

The guilt and anxiety came back. I had legitimately forgotten about the blood tests, at least the first time. After that? Well, I was secretly happy to be NEC and didn't want that to change. Perhaps I thought that if I didn't do the tests, then the cancer wouldn't come back. It was stupid, though—not testing for things doesn't mean they aren't there. I didn't want to go back to being a full-time sick person; I wanted to live my life. Isn't that a small enough thing to want?

"We have you booked in for a biopsy tomorrow at noon, and a PET scan the next morning. You'll follow up with me two days later—we'll have the results by then," she said. She handed me a card with the details of all the tests and appointments they had booked for me.

"I'll see you in a couple of days," the doctor said, turning and walking out.

Nurse Claire came in afterward and removed my IV, letting me know they were working on my discharge papers. They would allow Becca in to keep me company until they finished the paperwork.

When Becca came in, I couldn't help but smile.

"I'm sorry," I said. "I'll clean the bedroom as soon as I get home."

"You're sweet but clueless," she said, smiling at me with relief, wrapping her hand around mine and stroking the top with her thumb. "If you don't clean blood right away, it stains. I tried to save the bedroom, but the sheets, pillows, and mattress are beyond saving. I've already ordered a new mattress, it should be here tomorrow, and on the way home, we can pick out fresh sheets and pillows. I cleaned the floor, and the actual bed is safe, so at least it won't be too expensive to replace what got damaged."

"I'm sorry."

"Not your fault," she said.

"I didn't say it was my fault, I said I was sorry." I squeezed her hand.

"Yeah. I'm sorry, too."

"You won't believe this," I said, looking up at her from the bed. "But my doctor's name is Doctor Jones, like the Aqua song."

Becca giggled but then turned serious.

"Dr. Gillian called your parents; your mom wants us to call as soon as we leave the hospital. Your aunts said we can stay in their guest room until our mattress gets delivered."

"That was nice."

"She's family, Jer."

"Then you probably better stop calling her Dr. Gillian. After all, you're Dr. Rebecca now."

She smiled at me.

"Yeah. Family."

"Yeah... Look, I asked for them to let you see me, over and over, but they wouldn't."

"I know, they told me."

"It's not for lack of trying, I mean," I insisted.

"Jeremy," she kissed my cheek. "It's okay. We're family—we don't need the hospital's approval to make that true."

"Well, I'll have to look into a way to make you next of kin if this turns out to be something serious."

"Well, you could marry me," she laughed.

"I don't want to marry you just to allow you to see me in hospital; I want to marry you because I want to spend the rest of my life with you."

"The sap meter is running high," she said, but she blushed and smiled as she turned to look away, nevertheless.

"Do you want to marry me?" she asked. "I mean, eventually."

"Yeah. Do you want to marry me? Eventually?"

"Of course I do," she said, looking back at me.

I had a lot to think about now.

Mom wasn't impressed with me when I phoned her after the hospital finally discharged me.

"So, you've been having nosebleeds for how long?"

"Since we came back from Australia."

"And why haven't you had them looked at yet?"

"I dunno, Mom; they weren't that bad. Until last night, they only lasted for less than ten minutes, and I could control them. I thought it was from dry air or something."

"So, what are they doing about them?"

I sighed. "They're gonna do some tests. They cauterized the bleeds last night and gave me fluids."

"What tests?"

"Lots of blood tests. I'm seeing a hematologist."

"Have you booked a PET scan, over a year late, I might add?"

"Yes, and a bone marrow biopsy tomorrow."

"Jeremy, you need to do better. You know you have a higher risk of getting sick again. You need to stay on top of this stuff."

"Yeah, I know. I'll tell you how it goes. We're at Aunt Gillian's now. Gotta go."

"Take better care of my son."

I hung up the phone.

"We're not even close to Gillian's," Becca said, taking my left hand with her right and resting it on the center armrest of the car.

"I know," I said, sitting back in the seat and resting my head on the headrest and closing my eyes. "I know she's right," I said after a moment. "I was stupid. I should have listened to her and stayed on top of tests and check-ups."

"Yeah, you should have." She squeezed my hand.

"Yeah." I looked over at her, admiring her profile. "Well, I'm catching up now. Thing is, though, I don't know if it will make an actual difference. If something shows up, then I will be sick, whether it's found now or last year. God, I'm so sick of being sick, you know?"

"Yeah, I know. The would-haves and should-haves don't really matter now. What does is finding out why you're bleeding—that and checking everything to make sure you're still healthy. This is just a scare, that's all. Nothing to freak out about, right?"

"Yeah." I was all *'yeah's'* today.

"You're all 'yeah's; today," Becca said.

I squeezed her hand and laughed.

And like that, we drove into the mall parking lot. Considering I had ruined the sheets and pillows in the first place, I didn't object to the floral pattern Becca picked out—even if again, they looked suspiciously like the ones in which grandpa had died.

We bought them and then headed over to Aunt Gillian's.

She and Aunt Sam made us dinner, and we told them the rest of the details about our night in the hospital. Aunt Sam said she knew Dr. Jones, and she was good, which gave me some relief. She looked a bit worried about the test Dr. Jones ordered. I tried not to think about it too much.

The next day, Becca and I went home. I felt lucky that it was her weekend off—this would have been much harder on my own, although as soon as I thought it, I kicked myself. I was still feeling tired, even though I had slept a lot. Becca would have taken the time off, even if she had been scheduled to work.

Becca asked me if I wanted her to come to the clinic for the biopsy, but I said no—she should be home for when they delivered our new mattress, so we wouldn't need to ask Aunt G to spend another night in their guest room.

I'd had bone marrow biopsies before. Basically, it goes like this: You show up, and they make you change into a gown and lie flat on this bed. Then they stick a bunch of freezing chemicals into your ass and hip, and once it takes effect, they stick two needles into your bone. One draws out a vial of blood and fluid from your marrow, and the second removes a piece of the bone and the marrow. Getting the needle stuck into you sucks; they literally breaking your hip with a needle, and when they let the fluid out, the pain doubles. So, let's say it's like having your bone broken, and then the two ends stabbed together a bunch of times; it's all deep pressure and pain. When they are all done, you have to lie flat on your back for half an hour to make sure you don't bleed out. Then you have to put on loose pants that won't press on the bandage and wound, and you can't lift anything for a week. It sucks ass. Get it? Or should I say 'it's a pain in the ass?' Okay, humor aside—it was awful.

They send you for blood work immediately after getting the biopsy. They even push you in a wheelchair to the lab. So, I finally left with a hole in my butt and both arms. At least they let you drive as long as you're not bleeding and have taken the Tylenol they give you.

When I got home, the mattress was there; the delivery people even brought it upstairs. It was rolled up and vacuum-sealed in a box. Becca and I cut it open, and she lifted it onto the bed frame so we could cut open the plastic. Over the next couple of hours, the mattress inflated and hardened. I sat and tried to relax and recover. My hip throbbed with pain, and when I felt a bit better, I made dinner. Becca had finished making up the bedroom and cleaning up the plastic and debris by the time the food was ready.

After dinner, exhausted and sore, I went to bed. Becca climbed in beside me, and we spooned until I fell asleep. I had my hand on her hip, and the feeling of her across my chest and upper legs was reassuring and strong.

I tried not to think about what the outcome of the tests could be, but deep down, I knew that if it were cancer, things would become terrible quickly. It was the first time I allowed myself to consider that I might have cancer cells inside me again. Over time, I let myself come to accept that the life of a cancer victim might once again be my reality.

I woke up a lot during the night, both from pain and from just... unsettled dreams. They were what I call stress dreams, like you're running late for a flight, but no matter what you do, you can't go faster. Or you really have to make an appointment, but you can never reach the building because as fast as you go, people try to stop you, and you never get closer to where you need to be. I woke up more tired than I was when I went to bed.

They didn't want me to eat anything. I also had to drink a lot of water to make sure my stomach was empty, and my blood glucose was in the right range before my PET scan. Becca dropped me off at the hospital. She had wanted to come in with me, but I told her not to bother; she wouldn't be allowed to be with me the whole time I was getting the procedure done anyway, so she may as well go home and save on parking at the hospital. I had made up the couch before leaving so that I would have somewhere to sleep after the procedure; you're not supposed to sleep with or cuddle someone after you get the PET scan since you're radioactive for a day afterward. Since they want you to drink what feels like eight bottles of water an hour, the couch was also closer to the bathroom.

By now, I knew I wouldn't be turning into the Hulk from the radiation, though the idea of becoming a cancer-ridden superhero made me smile. I could have a grim sense of humor in these circumstances, right?

I walked into the nuclear medicine clinic. The layout was different from the one in Chicago, but they were essentially all the same. After handing over my ID to the receptionist, they gave me another bottle of water to drink, and I sat in the waiting room until they called. A lot of sick people sat in the waiting room. One man looked like he was on death's door, even though he was only maybe thirty-five; he reminded me of what I used to look like. I looked away and tried not to think about it.

The TV showed some evangelical Christian channel, and it seemed like the people on there knew they were being shown in a waiting room filled with desperate people. They seemed gleeful to have an audience of people who might not be thinking clearly to win over. Their sweet tone and gentle ministrations made me feel sick. I wondered why the hospital allowed this to be on the TV. It relieved me when one of the nurses finally turned it off.

"Jeremy?" a tech called.

"Yeah, that's me." I stood and walked down the hall to a compact room.

"Have a seat." The tech pricked my finger to check my blood glucose.

I got a Band-Aid for my finger, and the tech led me to another room—this one with a recliner and thick walls and a door. It was dimly lit. She handed me a heated gown and a bunch of heated blankets; shivering can cause false positives on the PET scan. Then she started the IV and wheeled in a cart covered with lead shielding. She hooked the cart up to my IV and set a timer. She left the room and closed the big door. With a hum, the machine pumped radioactive sugar into my blood; it didn't feel like anything. After the machine dosed me, which only took a minute or so, the tech came back in and gave the speech about how the test works.

"We gave you glucose because your body absorbs it well, especially if you don't have a lot in your blood to begin with. When it enters your body, any abnormal cells will eat the glucose faster than the rest, then they'll glow when we do the scan," she said. I already knew this, but it was reassuring to learn that the test's fundamentals hadn't changed in the last couple of years. I noticed the increased sarcasm and promised myself I wouldn't get carried away with it this time; I set my mind on trying to stay positive.

After turning off the machine and wheeling the cart out of the room, the technician took out my IV and gave me more blankets. Then I just sat in that room for forty-five minutes. I wasn't allowed to read or listen to my phone or anything, just sit still and let the sugar bind to any active cells in my body.

I tried not to think about what would happen if the results were positive. I closed my eyes and focused on breathing. In and out. In and out. Staying calm.

I must have dozed off because the next thing I knew, they knocked and came into the room to take me to the PET/CT scanner. I lay on the table, and it did its work. It's an enormous machine you move through, and it gives you about a thousand X-rays, looking for masses in your body and hot spots of radiation. When completed, I changed and threw my gown into a yellow bag with a big nuclear hazard symbol on it. I wondered if they would get treated and cleaned or treated as hazardous waste and thrown out.

The next two days dragged by. I worried my nose might start bleeding any time it twinged.

I went to class and tried to act like everything was normal; Becca and I even worked one night at the observatory.

"You okay, Jeremy?" Beth asked.

"No, not really. Been feeling sick, actually."

"Well, you sure look like you got run over by a steamroller." She gave me a hug. "You two let me know if you need anything, okay?"

We nodded and went outside to set up the telescopes. I got so into showing a bunch of school kids Jupiter that things felt normal. I forgot the dread of hanging on the edge of a cliff by one hand, ready to fall back down into the world of cancer.

The next day, I went to my doctor's appointment. It didn't go well. Not. At. All.

"Jeremy, how are you feeling?" Dr. Jones began.

"I don't know, why don't you tell me? I'm trying not to freak out."

"Well, I'll get right to it so that you don't have to freak out anymore. Your PET scan showed some areas of concern; you have masses in your sinuses and your stomach. However, the one that concerns me the most is next to your spine. It's difficult to say if it's on the bone or if it's touching the spinal cord at this point, but the good news is they are all relatively small. Going after them aggressively will help increase your quality of life and get you better faster."

Fuuuuuuuuck. It felt like someone had pulled the rug out from under me. They say that your life flashes before your eyes, but that's not what happened to me. My mind skipped ahead to Becca and me getting married, buying a house, getting a cat, traveling the world, and growing old together. And now none of that probably wouldn't happen. I wasn't scared of dying—I mean, we're all dead before we're born. No, what terrified me was thinking of leaving Becca, not being there for her, not being with her.

"So, how did I go from NEC to full-blown tumors in two-and-a-half years?" I said the dreaded T word since doctors always want to call them 'masses' because it sounds less scary.

"It's hard to say. Maybe when you had your surgery and last round of treatment, a few cancer cells may have survived. Since they were so small, they may not have been picked up on PET scans. They probably migrated and grew until now. The masses in your sinuses are the likely cause of your nosebleeds. Do you have any tingling, numbness, or weakness in your hips, legs, or feet?"

"No."

"Okay, that's an excellent sign that the mass on your spine likely isn't causing your spinal cord any issues right now."

"What's the plan?" I asked, dreading the answer.

"Well, I would suggest that we start you on chemotherapy, and use radiation therapy for your sinuses and spine. We can use chemo pills for the mass in your stomach. Surgery might still be an option. We will get you set up with an oncologist and a radiation oncologist, and together, we will work out the details and confirm everything."

I must have looked crushed. Either that or she had delivered this news so many times, she knew exactly what was going through my head. She said, "It's not too late. Yes, it would have been good if we had caught this earlier, but it's not hopeless. We will get you fixed up as best we can."

I left the clinic with even more booked appointments and tests; they had to confirm everything, after all.

I looked at my phone as I walked to my car—a bunch of missed calls from Mom. As I cleared the alerts, she called again. I declined the phone call and got into the car, but didn't start it. I felt like they had assaulted me, and that it was all my fault. Why hadn't I listened to my mom and booked my follow up PET scans? I was so stupid. Here I had, through sheer laziness and fear, probably gotten myself killed.

I sat behind the wheel of my car and cried, the phone continuing to buzz on the seat beside me. After pulling myself together, I set off for home, driving safe, paying extra attention to the road so I could keep my mind clear and let my emotions fade.

Becca was back at work starting that night, so she was asleep when I got home. I crept into the house and sat on the couch, processing the news. I felt my face and abdomen to see if I could feel any lumps in there. Of course I couldn't, but it felt like I could feel them inside me, taking on an awareness of something foreign and yet familiar.

When Becca woke a few hours later and came into the living room, she didn't need to ask. One look at her and I broke down in tears again. She cried as well, coming over and sitting on the floor in front of me. She took my hand and said, "It doesn't matter, Jeremy—we can get through this. You've done it before, so you know how to do it now. We will kick this cancer's ass even quicker this time."

I leaned my head against hers, and we sat together for a few minutes.

"I wanted to tell you first. I better call my mom now."

That didn't go well, either.

12

Becca picked me up from my first chemo session the following week.

I had allowed myself to sulk for one more day after getting the news. I made myself get up and get back into my routine. I had a touch of cancer—that didn't mean I couldn't still be out and enjoying life. Fresh attitude in hand, I went for a run at the school gym in the morning before class. Chemo would take a lot out of me, so I thought it better build my strength up as much as possible now. Becca and I also changed our diets to include more healthy food. She was always slim, but since I had packed on a few pounds in the last year, they fell away as I prepared myself for the fight ahead.

It was always surprising to me how much my mood influenced the experience of the world. I decided I would be in a good mood—positive and hopeful and making plans for the future, not putting everything on hold.

I went to the local barber to get my head shaved, much to Becca's chagrin. When she saw me with a bald head, she couldn't help but laugh.

"You look ridiculous," she said, giving me a hug.

I smiled. "If by ridiculous you mean totally hot and sexy, then yes, I agree."

She giggled. "Even cutting off all your hair isn't enough to make you ugly."

"As I said," I replied, "it's because I'm just naturally hot and sexy. Admit it—I'm exceptional."

She giggled again and punched me lightly on the arm. "Okay there, Narcissus."

The next night, we went back up Mars Hill for an observation night. We weren't working, which was strange for us.

Beth threw her arms around us when we walked through the door of the interpretation center.

"Beth!" Becca said in surprise. "What are you doing working a night event?"

"I normally don't, but I'm down two of my best employees at the moment." She glared at us with fake anger, then grinned. "It's nice to see you two. I had worried that you forgot about me up here on this hill."

"We could never do that," I said with a smile.

"After all, it's almost entirely your fault I ended up with this nut job," Becca teased, leaning into me and taking my hand.

"Okay, enough of the reunion, I've got guests to attend to. You guys have fun, and don't forget you promised to help me out every once in a while so I can get a night off."

"Didn't you hire some additional people?" Becca asked.

"Yeah, but they're not as good as you guys, so I have to monitor them closely," she said to us. She turned and shouted, "No, Charlie, you can't open the presentation room doors yet, they're still watching the film. We have a timer right there above the door!" She turned back to us. "See what I mean?"

Becca and I nodded and headed out to the observatory grounds as Beth ran to correct another new staff member.

The cool autumn night felt refreshing as Becca and I walked arm in arm up the slight incline of the path towards the crown of the hill. The red footlights made the path glow with a peaceful shade of red, preserving our night vision.

"Where do you want to start?" I asked her.

"Let's see what they have on the eight-inch telescopes and work our way around from there, ending at the Clark."

"Sounds good."

Saturn showed on all the small telescopes. Saturn's cool; most people want to see it, which is why they had it tying up so many telescopes, but I was a little disappointed in the lack of variety among the eight-inch scopes.

We walked over to the Clark and, to my delight, they had it on the Orion Nebula. We took our turns looking through the telescope at the blue and purple glow where stars are born. I remembered my second night in Flagstaff, when

Becca and I had gone to 'make-out point' on the drive up the hill and had looked out at the stars. She had pointed this nebula out to me. One odd thing for many visitors was that when they leave the Clark, they have to walk by Percival Lowell's tomb. Becca and I stopped at the grave and gave our respects. I thought about loving a place so much you want to be buried there and then tried desperately not to think about it.

Chemo went exactly as I expected. They bring you into this room with lots of Lazy Boy-type chairs, sit you down, hook you up to a machine, and pump poison into you. You just hope that you get the cancer before the chemo gets you.

Since this was my first round of chemo, I didn't feel any side effects yet. In a few days, though, I'd feel crappy. As I said, it was poison.

So when that was over, I jumped in the car with Becca, and we headed out of town. Beth had let us use her campsite again, and we wanted a night to relax before I would start to feel sick the following day.

I was very nervous.

About an hour after we left Flagstaff, we pulled into the camping site with which we were so familiar. I set up the tent while Becca moved the firewood. I was still strictly forbidden from lifting anything heavy for a few more days, so she wouldn't let me help her, even after I offered.

As the sun set into the cool fall evening, we cuddled close, shoulder to shoulder, by the fire.

"I know this is a terrible time to be asking this," I said after the sun had set and the stars filled the night sky. "But I just can't wait anymore."

Becca turned to look at me inquisitively.

"I'm not asking you now because of anything to do with my health. I am asking because I love you and want to spend the rest of my life with you. Becca, I love you more than all the stars in the sky. More than I've ever thought I could ever love anyone."

"Um, Jeremy...?" Becca asked. I detected a slight shake in her voice.

"Will you... Will you do me the honor.... Will you marry me?" There. I had done it. I pulled out a small ring with an opal in it from my pocket and held it up for her to see.

"YES! Of course I will!" She threw herself at me, and we flopped back onto the ground, lips locked.

After we had come up for air, I gave her grandma's pendant. She read the note, and we both teared up.

Becca pulled me up and toward the tent.

"Like our first time," she said.

"You sure it's a good idea? The chemo will start to come out through my saliva and stuff soon. I don't want it to poison you, too." Chemo side effects are no joke.

"Doctors orders," she said with a wink.

"You're the doctor," I said with a laugh, letting her guide me toward the tent.

It was like the first time all over again, except this time, when I got naked, my scars weren't something I was ashamed of. I felt like I would never grow tired of Becca's hungry look when she saw me naked. I knew I would never tire of her slim hips, her small and perfectly proportioned breasts, or the flush of lovemaking on her cheeks.

I nudged her legs apart, and this time, as my tongue wrote out our names on her clit, I combined our last names, like what might happen when we get married. It was like she could feel it too because she came quickly as my tongue danced and my fingers caressed her sides and nipples.

Being hard as a rock, I crawled up, kissing her as I went; hips, belly button, all over the breasts, collar bone, neck, lips, eyes, cheeks. My probing penis found the correct angle, and I plunged inside her. The familiar warm and tight feeling engulfed me. It was like dialing in a combination on a lock—pleasant and tactile until suddenly, the lock springs opened, and everything fell out. My cum flooded into her as she dialed in the last digit on my metaphorical lock. We shuddered together in perfect harmony. I grew limp inside her, while inside me the cancer felt the first brushes of poison and fought back.

By the time my third chemo treatment came around, I was feeling the side effects—vomiting, weakness, weight loss, pain all over my body...everything you can think of.

They also mixed in radiation treatment. Radiation differs from chemo. They lay you on a cold table and shoot radiation into you. It's like getting an X-ray, only thousands of them. They hope the chemo and the radiation will kill the cancer. There were days where I could work, and days where I couldn't. I ended up dropping most of my academic classes but kept plugging away at my thesis. I would do this round of chemo by the end of the semester. If things went well, I could resume classes in the spring semester, and I would only be one semester behind. At least, that was the plan.

Becca kept working her usual rotation, and we tried to live a happy and normal life.

A normal life, in our case, also involved planning a wedding.

"So, I'm thinking spring break?" Becca mused at one of our wedding planning meetings.

"I was hoping for sooner."

"Jer, it's already almost December—I don't think we can make it happen any faster. It takes time to book and plan for these sorts of things."

"We could elope. Get on a plane somewhere and do it."

"Like a destination wedding?"

"Sure!"

"Are you sure it's a good idea for you to travel?"

"Not at all. We could do Vegas, though—that's not too far."

"Really? Vegas? What little girl dreams about getting married in Vegas?"

"I don't think I'm qualified to answer questions about what girls think," I said with a laugh. "Let alone what little girls think."

She grinned at me from across the table.

An idea struck me.

"We could do it at the observatory?" I asked. "I mean, we would have to ask Beth if we could rent out the library or something. Or do it in the Clark dome."

"You know, that's not a bad idea," Becca said. "I mean, I don't know about doing it under the Clark, but that would be hilarious. We'll have to ask Beth. But still, I can't see getting it all together until March."

As Becca leaned forward to look at some papers, I caught a glimpse down her shirt. Aside from noticing she wasn't wearing a bra, I saw that she was wearing my grandmother's pendant. My grandmother had a fantastic sense of humor. I think she would laugh at the thought of her pendant caressing the sides of Becca's bare breasts, given how prudish everyone else was about nudity on that side of the family—I know that I appreciated it. Lost in my thoughts, I missed something Becca had said.

"Huh?"

"My eyes are up here, Jeremy," she said with a pretend scowl.

"Sorry, I was enjoying the view."

She laughed. "So, spring break?"

"Sure—sounds like a date," I smiled. Even though I wasn't feeling all that good physically, I still felt content.

"We're supposed to work the viewing night in a couple of days; we can talk to Beth then. We need to think about what we'll wear, invitations, meals, guest list, et cetera."

"You mean my tux T-shirt isn't good enough?" I teased.

Becca had taken a drink, and water came out of her nose as she cracked up. I loved that I still made her smile, even after all this time together.

A few days later, we got to the observatory early to make sure we would see Beth before she went home.

"Hey Beth, before you go, do you have a second?"

"Sure, Jeremy, what's up?"

"Jeremy and I are planning out our wedding…" Becca started.

"OOOOO," Beth squealed. "You set a date then?"

"Not quite yet," I replied, shooting Becca a wink. "We wanted to have it here, so we figured we would ask if there's a night available and cheap we could book, and then that would be the date."

"You two are too cute," Beth said. "Listen, you can pick any evening we don't have a scheduled event, and you can book it for free, so long as you meet my two conditions."

"What are they?" Becca asked.

"The first one is I need you two to work next Tuesday all day—I need a day off, and it's a viewing night. No one else is available."

"We can make that happen," Becca said, looking at me. I nodded.

"What's the second condition?" I asked.

"Invite me, obviously!"

Venue problem solved, we had to figure out the guest list. Becca and I had both wanted to keep the attendance low.

"I reckon just Mom and Abby," Becca said. "And obviously Beth and Gillian and Sam."

"Okay. Probably just Mom and Dad on my side."

"You aren't going to invite your sisters?"

"I wasn't planning to."

"Jeremy, you should."

"But they're brats," I said with a laugh.

"You haven't seen them in over two years. You should invite them."

I caved. I drafted up invitations on my computer and printed them. We dropped the ones that had to go out of town off at the post office and hand-delivered the local invitations.

The New Year came and went. I was growing skinnier and looking gaunter. I was also feeling weaker, and I slept more and more. I decided only to take two classes for the spring semester, banking on feeling better once this round of chemo finished mid-January.

When the chemo finished, I had another PET scan. The tumors hadn't shrunk, but they hadn't grown, either. They say no news is good news, but that's not really true—this didn't answer any questions. Was the treatment stopping the cancer's growth? Who knows? Was the cancer even responding to the treatment? Maybe it's just growing slowly? I couldn't tell you. I sighed.

"We'll have to do another round of chemo, with some different medicine in it for this go around," Dr. Jones said.

"When will it start?" I asked, resigned.

"Well, I'd like to give you six weeks off, so you can have some time to recuperate from this round. I think we should start the next in mid-March. We can continue with radiation treatment, meanwhile. How have the nosebleeds been?"

"I still get them, but nothing like when I had to go to the ER. I still have trouble breathing through my nose; it's like I'm permanently stuffy."

"But no real change?"

"Not really."

"Okay. Well, we'll get you booked for another PET scan a week before we start chemo. I'll see you in March."

Before I knew it, it was the day of our wedding. Mom, Aunt G, Sam, Abby, and Gwen had taken over our house, kicking me, Dad and the twins out to spend the day at Aunt G's. I had picked up my rental tuxedo the day before at the mall. It had been a challenge to find one that would fit me because of the weird weight loss on some parts of my body from the chemo. My shoulders still had muscle, but my waist was much smaller, so anything that fit my shoulders looked like a bag over the rest of me.

Dad drove us to the observatory in the evening after I had showered, shaved, and changed into the tux. Everyone else would meet us there. I was nervous; I don't know why, as this was something I wanted, had planned for, but I knew that in an hour, my life would change forever.

We had the ceremony in the courtyard between the visitor center and the library. Aunt Gillian had made decorations that looked planets; they seemed to hover over a pot of white lilies that marked an aisle up the walkway from the visitor center. My dad and I walked up the aisle and stood next to the officiant. Everyone stood together in clusters on either side of the aisle. I saw the door to the visitor center open, and Abby walked out in a brilliant blue dress holding a bouquet of the white lilies. Behind her, I saw a flash of white and knew it was about to happen. Phil Collins' song, 'You'll be in my heart' began playing, and it started.

When Becca walked toward me, I couldn't help but cry. I had seen her in her dress before—heck, I had been there when she tried them on and had to help her decide which one to get. But still, here she was. I felt drunk, like I was watching this happen to someone else through my tears, but it wasn't happening to someone else. When she reached me, I took her hand, looking down into her brown eyes and smiling, cheeks damp. She squeezed my hand, and we turned to face the officiant.

"Good evening and welcome," the officiant began. "Jeremy and Rebecca chose the words you are about to hear. You have known each other from the first glance of acquaintance to this point of commitment," she continued.

My mind returned to the first time I had seen Becca and what an uncomfortable and awkward person I was back then. I remembered being star-struck by her beauty, and how I had shocked her with static electricity while she stood next to Beth in the visitor center. I looked at her now and felt the same breath catch, heart skip a beat, giddy with excitement that I had felt then. If I'm honest, I felt like that every time I looked at her. How fitting that we were marrying where it all began.

"All those conversations that begin with 'when we are married,' and continue with 'I will and you will and we will'…"

I turned back to what the officiant was saying before getting lost again. Becca had warned me I wouldn't hear very much of the actual ceremony—she was so right.

"The symbolic vows you are to make are a way of saying to one another, 'You know all those things that we've promised and hoped and dreamed? Well, I meant it. Every word.'

"Repeat after me," the officiant said. Becca squeezed my hand and pulled me from my fog.

"I call upon those present to witness that I, Jeremy, do take you, Rebecca, to be my lawful wedded wife. I will love you faithfully through the difficult and the easy. I promise to laugh with you, cry with you, and grow with you. I promise to support your dreams, and to respect our differences, and to love you and be by your side through all the days of our lives. As I have given you my hand to hold, I give you my heart to keep."

"I call upon those present to witness that I, Rebecca, do take you, Jeremy, to be my lawful wedded husband. I will love you faithfully through the difficult and the easy."

There would be difficulty ahead—just a touch of cancer for me to get through.

"I promise to laugh with you, cry with you, and grow with you."

I thought back to all the times we had spent laughing together; the night we both cried when I got my cancer diagnosis.

"I promise to support your dreams, and to respect our differences, and to love you and be by your side through all the days of our lives."

I sure hope I would give her a long time to live up to that promise we made to each other.

"As I have given you my hand to hold, I give you my heart to keep."

I looked into the depths of her eyes, and we smiled, each of us with tears rolling down our cheeks.

"You have kissed a thousand times, maybe more. But today, the feeling is new. No longer simply partners and best friends, you will soon become husband and wife and will seal the agreement with a kiss. Today, your kiss is a promise."

"And now, by the power vested in me by the State of Arizona, I pronounce you husband and wife."

And that was that. Surrounded by friends, family, telescopes, and history, we were finally, irrefutably married in front of the library on top of Mars Hill. I was so ready. As I looked at Becca's brilliant smile, I knew she was, too. And I couldn't have been happier.

We went over to Aunt G's house after the wedding. She had a big backyard; she had rented outdoor heaters because it was still cold at night, and we had a little party. Becca drove us from the observatory down to Aunt G's since I was not fit to drive after having taken some painkillers. I would go for days or weeks feeling great and healthy, and then one or two days of feeling like I'd been kicked repeatedly all over my body. Now that the nerves and excitement of marrying Becca were over, the assault of being sick took over. The pills dulled the pain a little. I looked over at Becca and knew that the best thing that would ever happen to me already had and that I could now live forever with the very best person I knew. Even if my cancer were cured tomorrow, this would still outshine any feelings of joy caused by that.

As we drove down the winding road from the observatory, with the trees whipping by us as we descended, I pulled myself together for what was to come. I looked over to Becca again, driving us in her dress. She wore the safety boots she kept in the car, the white sandals that she wore during the wedding sitting upside down on her lap. Her white dress had a floral pattern over her waist and chest that showed her curves just right. The lower half was a kind of long flowing lace. I didn't know enough about clothes to identify everything with proper names; the only thing that mattered is that she loved the dress. I knew I didn't have to tell anyone that she looked beautiful in it because she would look beautiful in a paper bag.

We were the last to arrive at Aunt Gillian's.

Mom and Dad met Gwen and Abby. Dad was making Becca's family laugh when we opened the door and walked in. Soon enough, I was sure they would be swapping stories about Becca and me growing up.

Aunt G had transformed her dining room and living room into a party space. A fire was going, and they had set two seats up across the room facing it. Someone had pinned cloth signs to the chairs, which read 'Bride' and 'Groom.'

Becca and I circled the room and thanked everyone for coming. Then I cued my Dad, and he played 'Yellow' by Coldplay on the stereo. Becca and I danced. After that, it was time to cut the cake. This all went by in a blur to me. I kept squeezing Becca's hand to make sure it was all real; she would squeeze back and smile at me.

Finally, we had time to sit down, which was great because I felt dizzy—probably from the painkillers. My aunts took care of serving the cake to everyone. I picked at it but couldn't imagine eating anything, so I relaxed on the chair next to Becca and sipped on some water; everyone else had beer or champagne. Becca was ecstatic, her smile cutting through the crowd like the beam of a lighthouse on a foggy day. The last time I had seen her anywhere near being so happy was when I had given her the tickets to Australia.

Aunt G's cat, Luthien, jumped up into my lap and lay on my legs against my belly, purring. It was as if she knew my stomach wasn't feeling well, and she was trying to help me. I rubbed behind her ears and along her back, and she closed her eyes in contentment.

Becca looked down at the cat and then up at me. "Grandkitties," she whispered at me. I chuckled and nodded. I kept it together for a few more hours until the party wound down.

Soon, everyone went back to where they were staying, and Becca and I went home. Exhausted, I fell into bed while Becca cleaned off the makeup she had worn and washed her hair. I tried to stay awake long enough to cuddle at least, but it seemed like I was asleep before my head hit the pillow.

I felt much better in the morning, back to my body tricking me into feeling like nothing was wrong. I knew from last time that this was just the beginning. Soon, the days of feeling sick would increase, and the days of feeling good would decrease until I had the last good day. If nothing else changed, eventually, it would be the end.

We hung out with our families for a few days. Dad had rented a van so we could all squeeze in. Becca and I showed them the giant meteor crater outside town and took them for a night to Grand Canyon National Park.

My family went home first, then Becca's. Then it was over.

My chemo started the day after they left. Six weeks had gone by in a flash. The chemo round started the same as the last, feeling good for a few days and then starting to feel bad. Becca had driven with Gwen and Abby to LA with a stop in Vegas for the girls, so I was on my own for a few days. I went to class, led a seminar, worked on my thesis, and my doctor poisoned me repeatedly.

When she got home, Becca and I settled back into our routine. The routine of our married life was an awful lot like the one of our engaged life and of our boyfriend/girlfriend life. The only actual difference was I referred to her as my wife now, and when we took a shower, we had to take off and put on our rings.

I registered Becca as my next of kin on my insurance and emergency contact forms at school and the hospital. They finally allowed her to sit with me during chemo. It was nice to have her there, to talk to and joke with while I spent time hooked up to the machine that tried to save my life.

A few weeks later, we had to file our first taxes as a married couple—something we had to spend an entire week figuring out how to do. We used our tax refund to go on a honeymoon; we went in a time between my chemo treatments. My doctors said I could travel, but they warned me to make sure I had ready access to medical care, just in case. And also try not to get sick and to stay somewhere with western medicine.

We had debated going to Chicago to visit my family. Becca was in favor of it, and so was my mom, but I wanted our honeymoon to be somewhere special and just for us.

We chose New York City and Washington, DC; both were historic cities, which appealed to me. Both had great science attractions, like the Hayden Planetarium and the Air and Space museum for Becca. We had a fantastic time on the trip; we even saw a few shows on Broadway that my Aunts insisted I couldn't miss, no matter what. The planetarium was great, although we didn't bump into Neil de Grasse Tyson, as I kind of hoped we would. We watched a show where you start at the planetarium, and over the next few minutes, pull out to the edge of the universe and then zoom back in. That was neat to see. We also saw the usual star talk planetarium shows that you would typically expect to see. DC was an emotional experience, too, telling Becca about all the history that had happened there. We spent a night walking along the mall, stopping at the war memorials, and standing on the spot where Martin Luther King Jr said, "I have a dream." It was like when I was a kid all those years ago, but instead of being on a trip with my dad, I got to share it all with Becca.

And time went on, spring turning to summer. I kept getting worse. My tumors had grown again. They thought about surgery to try to remove the one in my stomach but decided that getting the one on my spine and in my sinuses was too risky. Instead, they increased the chemo dose and the pace of radiation therapy.

Becca tried not to show me that she was growing worried about my deteriorating health. I tried to stay positive; I'd been through this before. Last time, it got way worse than this before it got better. And like I thought, it kept getting worse.

13

By summer, I was gaunt and weak, close to what I had looked like last time, before I got better. I hoped I would begin to get better soon, but so far, there was no sign of it happening.

Becca helped—a lot. But when I looked at her, I felt guilty. I was spiraling downward and had dragged her into it. I had married her when I knew I was very sick. I also knew I was being an idiot. She knew that things might not go the way we wanted. I also knew that if she were sick instead of me, I would be there for her as much as she was for me. I hoped for a someday where I could be there for her, unconditionally and lovingly, to show her how much her help meant to me.

She kept excelling in her career. They had already given her full funding for an extra project. She couldn't tell me what it was, but she had flown around the country, giving briefings to scholars and military brass. I was so proud of her.

I went to work, excited for her to come home from one of these trips. I got to my office and graded some papers before heading out for lunch with my advisor. I went over how things were going. She gave me some tips on research and writing techniques that would help to improve the draft of the thesis I had turned in. I was happy I was making some progress on it and thought about how I would incorporate that advice into my draft. I had only ordered a salad, but when it came, I wasn't hungry. I picked at it while Dr. Jansen ate her sandwich; the look of the food was nauseating to me. I didn't want to seem rude, so I ate a small bit of lettuce. I felt it going down my throat and make a sickening splash as it entered my stomach. I immediately gagged.

"Excuse me," I said, turning to go to the men's room.

I pushed through the door and staggered toward the sink, heaving; no chance of making it to the toilet. I threw up. Red and watery vomit filled the sink. I threw up again. More red, with a lone piece of lettuce floating in the sink. Again. And again. I felt lightheaded, and my last thought was of hitting the blood-covered floor.

I woke up in the ICU. Wires were attached to my chest. I had two IV lines, one in each arm, attached to big bags of fluids. A steady beep of the cardiac monitor assured me I was still alive. I fumbled with both hands, looking for the call button. They always had it hooked over the bed rails somewhere within easy reach so you could let the nurses know when you woke up. I finally found it and pressed the big red button on its surface.

Mars Hill

Within seconds, a nurse came in to check up on me. I tried to sit up, but a tearing pain ripped through my abdomen, and I flopped back down.

"Don't try to move on your own, that's going to hurt a lot. Let me help you," the nurse said, lifting the head of my bed a few inches so that I was no longer prone.

"How long have I been out?" I asked.

"About three days," he said. I looked past him and out of the window, which I could now see. Through the glass, I saw office towers and a sprawling city.

"Phoenix?" I asked.

"Yeah, the hospital in Flagstaff had you helicoptered down here once they decided that the only way to stop the bleeding was to remove the tumor on your stomach. The doctors up there felt that you would do better having one of our doctors do the surgery since we do this kind of thing far more often than they do."

"Did anyone call my wife?"

"Yes, we pulled your next of kin information from your insurance company. She's been here but went to take a nap a few hours ago at her hotel. Do you want me to call her and let her know you're awake?"

I sighed with relief, sinking into the bed and collecting my thoughts.

"No, let her sleep. Do you have my phone? I'll text her. How did the surgery go?"

"They got most of the tumor, but, unfortunately, they found another one while they scanned you. I'll have to get the doctor to give you more information—they should be doing rounds in an hour. We locked your phone and your valuables at the nurses' station. I'll grab them for you now that you're awake."

The nurse left, and I stared out the window until I had my phone back and texted Becca. I had been hoping that the surgery would help fix me like last time. The thought occurred to me then that it hadn't cured me; this was the same bout of cancer I had last time.

Hours later, the surgeon came into the room to look at my incision and make sure it was healing okay. I didn't notice the wait too much since I spent most of the time sleeping. The nurses checked in on me regularly. It made time turn into a kind of slippery thing where you know it's passing, and you feel like it's both taking forever and no time at all. The surgeon told me that during an after surgery scan, they had noticed another tumor—this time on my heart. He said he was sorry to have to deliver that news, and that after a few more days of observation, they would send me back to Flagstaff; the doctors there would give me more information on my options. They would transfer me out of the ICU and into a regular ward in the morning if things went well overnight.

Becca came by that evening.

"I got your text. How are you feeling?" she asked softly.

"Like a gigantic bag of shit."

"You scared me."

"I'm sorry. I just really wanted to ride in a helicopter."

She gave me a small feeble smile at the joke. "Did they say when you would get to go home?"

"Another day or so."

"Okay. Do you want me to stay?"

"God, of course I do. I want you to be with me and never leave me alone again. But my practical side says it's stupid for you to spend money on a hotel, or drive an eight-hour round trip only to get to spend fifteen minutes with me before they kick you out. I'll be fine, and if anything happens, I'll call you. Shit, I'll probably be texting you every couple of minutes because I miss you too much."

She sat with me for the rest of the fifteen minutes they would allow someone to visit in the ICU. She kissed me and promised to text me when she got home. This hospital was super old-fashioned. Most hospitals were much more relaxed about their visitation policies. I stayed awake playing games on my phone until Becca sent me a text when she got home, and we texted for most of the night. I dozed, but the pain in my belly from the surgery kept me from getting a good night's sleep.

Three days later, they let me go. Becca and I had constantly been texting, as I promised. Every chance I got, I took a silly picture of me, or one of what I was doing. Becca sent me pictures of her getting the room ready at home, cooking and doing chores, teaching, and around town. I don't know what people did before text messages because I swear they kept me sane while I waited to get out of there. Becca drove down and picked me up to take me home. She gave me a light meal before I fell asleep, exhausted. There's something about being in your own bed that makes you able to sleep better.

I saw Dr. Jones a few days later.

"Look, Jeremy, it seems like nothing we're doing is working. Your most recent scan from Phoenix shows new tumors on your heart, liver, colon, and hip. The tumors we already knew about are growing again."

"Okay, so what can we do to cure me?"

She looked down at her desk, took a breath, and then looked back up at me.

"I'm sorry. You probably only have another four to six weeks. We can offer you palliative chemotherapy to help you feel okay, but there's very little chance we will cure this. I'll keep looking for any new drug or trial we can get you into, but if I can't find anything..."

Becca and I cried all night. Then I called my parents, and the crying started all over again. I kept apologizing to Becca. I loved her so much. I didn't want her to hurt from me dying. I had promised her a life with me, and now I felt like I was breaking my word.

I took the palliative chemo. It surprised me how good it made me feel—not good as in cured, but good as in no actual pain. I felt healthy, even as my body kept wasting away.

My parents decided to fly into town to be with Becca and me. On our last night alone before they flew in, I asked Becca if we could go camping again one last time.

"Jer, I'm not sure that's such a good idea," Becca said, as she was getting things ready for my parents to stay on our couch. She had pulled out and washed another sheet set and was grabbing some extra pillows before making it up into a bed.

"It probably isn't, but this will be our last night alone until my parents leave, and it's going to be a beautiful, warm, cloudless night."

Becca protested for another few minutes until she finally agreed and called Beth, who said we were welcome to use the campsite if we wanted. Becca packed our sleeping bags and tent into the car, and we headed out as the sun set. A pair of rabbits scurried across the road in the glare of our lights and disappeared into the grass on the other side.

I felt peaceful as I sat back and watched the view as we drove, the sun casting long shadows and illuminating the treetops and grass bright red.

"Are you going to be okay without me?" I asked Becca.

"Jeremy, I'm driving," she answered with a raspy voice as if she had a sore throat.

I reached out and took her hand. She squeezed mine. I turned and looked at her in profile. Her eyes were fixed on the road, and she looked exhausted. I looked down at our hands, hers as elegant and beautiful as ever, mine looking like a skeleton surrounded by a translucent material.

I won't be much food for the worms in this condition, I thought to myself. As I had grown sicker, my humor had become decidedly darker. I made sure not to voice these musings out loud; Becca would not appreciate hearing them.

I looked at her cheeks and admired the rosy bloom on them. Sliding my eyes down her body, I fantasized at what lay under her T-shirt. No matter how many times I saw her, I never tired of seeing her. I still couldn't believe she was mine. I felt the same excitement and desire that I had felt on my first day at Lowell when she walked through the door, and it felt like my life had changed. Of course, it had, but at the time I didn't know it.

Soon, Becca turned into the campsite. The familiar gate, walk to the fire pit, set up the tent, build the fire.

We watched the sunset and sat under blankets around the fire, the smoke blowing straight up before being caught by the wind, carrying it away into the darkness.

I leaned against her, and she wrapped her arm around mine, holding my hand. I felt the ring she wore as it pressed on my fingers.

"Thanks for bringing me out here. I doubt we would get another night alone once Mom comes."

"It's nice to be out with you; like our first time."

"Just like our first time," I agreed.

We sat like that, silent, watching the stars blossom into life above us, hearing and smelling the sweetness of the surrounding grasses, mixed with the distinctive and strong smell of the wood fire.

"What do you think happens when we die?" Becca asked me.

"I think the people who love us most will miss us," I replied. Becca rarely spoke about death around me.

After a minute, she pulled the blanket around the two of us.

I felt warm and oddly happy.

"I'll have to remember to tell Mom about you not knowing that there was free champagne on our flight to Australia," I said.

She laughed at the memory. "I still can't believe you made that trip happen for me."

"Of course I did—how else would I be able to join the mile-high club with the prettiest girl above, on, and dare I say under the earth's surface?"

"Oh, I think you dare," she said with a chuckle.

I breathed deeply. She turned and kissed me on the cheek. I turned and caught her lips; they tasted sweet from her lip gloss. She always wore the red lip gloss that tasted like berries when it was cold out. I wondered why I hadn't notice before now.

"Do you want to go to sleep?" she asked. We both knew that having sex was out of the question—I still excreted poison from my last dose of chemo, and I couldn't, even if I had wanted to; I was too weak for it. I just didn't want to admit it to her or myself.

"No. I want to stay out here with you."

"I love you, Jeremy," she said, kissing me again.

I looked up again at the band of light, composed of millions and millions of stars. A bright one caught my eye, and I wondered how far away it was. I felt myself growing tired, but I was warm under the blanket, even though the night had turned cold. I felt light.

"I love you too," I said. "I bet Mom and Dad will want to invite Aunt Gillian and Aunt Sam over for dinner. I think I'll make a roast. We'll have to get some more groceries on our way home."

"Sounds like a plan," Becca smiled at me, but with watery eyes. We both knew there was no way I could cook a roast; I could barely move on my own.

"Glad you think so."

"You know I always liked your cooking, but your roast is just... fantastic."

"I'll be sure to put extra love in it."

"You say that every time."

"And I mean it every time."

"You sound like a grandmother."

"I can't help it," I said.

"Sure you can't."

We lay back, holding hands and looking at the stars above us. My mind wandered back to the very first time we had looked at the stars. It felt like a lifetime ago, at the lookout just outside the observatory. I had felt awkward and childish then, barely comfortable being with the most beautiful woman in the world. I didn't understand that I was in for the greatest adventure one can have—falling in love. I regretted nothing other than that in a day or a week or two—or if I were lucky, six or seven months—I would be dead. And Becca would be alone without me again. But the time we had left to share, and the time we had already spent together would be amazing. It felt like every day we learned something new, told a joke, or shared a smile that was unique and valuable and precious.

I looked into the infinite depths of the sky above my head and again thought back to seeing Orion with Becca that first day, and I laughed.

Becca turned on her side and looked at me.

"What's so funny?"

"I was thinking about Orion."

"What about Orion?" she asked with a bit of a catch in her throat.

I turned toward her and smiled.

"Just that I wish Orion were up this time of year. I would have liked to see his junk one more time."

Becca smiled but didn't laugh.

"Remember how you explained about the sword on the first day we met? And that people said it was in the wrong place for a sword, so it was his dick?"

"Yeah. I remember."

We turned back to look up at the stars again. My vision was dark around the edges, but that made the stars right above us shine brighter. Time seemed to slow down, each second taking longer than the last. I was okay with it; it was more time for me to be with her.

"When you told me that, I... Well, I guess that's when I first thought you might be the person I would marry. Beautiful, smart, funny, and always making me want to be with you more. I love you, Becca, more than all the stars in the sky."

"Jeremy..." she said, now crying for real. "I love

EPILOGUE

Jeremy made it through that night; I was as surprised as anyone. I rushed him back into town and straight to the hospital. He was in the ICU for a week and the hospital for another two after that. Doctor Jones told me he was lucky to be alive. Against all odds, as the weeks went on, he put on weight and became stronger. I sat by his side as his parents flew in, and then they went home again; we never did have that roast beef dinner. When Jeremy came home, I stopped and got him shawarma, and we ate it in bed together. It made a mess, but we didn't care.

I expected to lose him any day, but he seemed determined to stay with me.

"Becca," he would say, "I promised you for better or worse, and since we've been married, it's been worse. I want to show you better."

"Jer, you're always better. You just have a touch of cancer, that's all. I regret nothing." I would say back.

This isn't one of those stories where he suddenly finds a miracle cure. He got well enough to get into a drug trial; it gave him two more years. He lived long enough to see Abby get married and then be the godfather to her daughter. We had a couple more scares where I thought I would lose him, but then he pulled through for another day. Another week. Another month.

Jeremy would spend a lot of time in his study when we were at home. I asked him what he was doing, but he always said I'd know soon. I was working at the observatory and on my own projects, so I let him do whatever it was he was doing.

He finally called me over and showed me what he was working on.

"I've been writing it down. Our story."

It took all my strength not to cry at that.

"I hope it's a long book," I told him.

He just laughed with his cute goofy grin.

He wrote every day, and every night I would come home and see where he was at with it. One night I came home, and he was gone. I found him leaning back in his chair with his eyes closed, his breath still and his hands on the keyboard, the story left at the point where I thought I had lost him for the first time.

That's the thing about death; it happens to you in the middle of your life. It doesn't care about your plans, who you love, or what you have left to live for. I don't think anyone is ever ready for death. You always have a plan for tomorrow, a dream you haven't fulfilled. Someone who you need to say, 'I love you' to one last time. You're never ready for tomorrow not to come, for the story to end. Life doesn't really have happy endings because real life isn't a story.

But if it was, then now I get to choose the ending. I get to be the hero's love interest. I get to have the romance you can only find in stories. I get to marry my best friend, to share a life with him. I get to wake up next to him every day, to laugh and smile and hold him. Of all the people for me to have met, I got to meet him. I got to be with him right to the end. And to me, that's a happy ending, no matter how long or how short the story is.

Rebecca van Wilde

Made in the USA
Coppell, TX
15 December 2021